Praise for J. M. Forster

Shadow Jumper

'Fantastically exciting. A GOLD MEDAL WINNER!'

The Wishing Shelf Book Awards

'Perfect for both teens and preteens.

Families Rating 6 out of 6.'

Families Online

'A tale full of adventure and mystery . . . with direct, accessible

language . . . A warm, human tale of friendship.'

Primary Times, Gloucestershire

D0263941

Also by J. M. Forster

Shadow Jumper: a mystery adventure for children and young teens. Available in paperback, ebook and audio download.

jm-forster.co.uk

jm-forster.com

Bad Hair Days

J. M. Forster

Copyright © J. M. Forster 2017

Published by Scribblepad Press 2017

All rights reserved.

ISBN: 978-0-9930709-2-1

No parts of this publication may be reproduced, stored in a retrieval system, or transmitted in any form or by any means, electronic, mechanical, photocopying, recording, or otherwise, without the prior written permission of the copyright owner.

This book is sold subject to the condition that it shall not, by way of trade or otherwise, be lent, resold, hired out, or otherwise circulated without the publisher's prior consent in any form of binding or cover other than that in which it is published and without a similar condition including this condition being imposed on the subsequent purchaser. Under no circumstances may any part of this book be photocopied for resale.

This is a work of fiction. Any similarity between the characters and situations within its pages and places or persons, living or dead, is unintentional and coincidental.

To my boys.

All four of them.

THINGS NOT TO DO:

1. Sleepovers (back-to-front hair is not a good look).

2. Shopping with mates (so many chances for wig discovery).

3. Rollercoasters and windy places (will my wig come off?).

4. Swimming (ditto).

5. Visiting the hair salon (no hair, no point).

Chapter One

Injections: check.

Ultraviolet light treatment: check.

Steroid creams – two types: check . . .

Dr Violetta listed the treatments I'd tried. Two of them had made no difference at all; the others had only worked for a few weeks. Going to the surgery made me grumpy and sad. There was never any good news. Ever.

'Is it worth trying injections again?' Mum asked the doctor.

'As I've said before, the problem is that once you stop them, Mallow's hair will fall out again, unless her own immune system kicks into action normally. But as you know, the course of the condition is unpredictable. And with large areas . . . *mutter* . . . ineffective . . . *mutter* . . . resolves

1

itself . . . hair growth . . . spontaneously.'

So. Nothing more to be done. That was what Dr Violetta was saying. I switched off. All I could think about was the message I'd received on my mobile earlier.

F•R•E•A•K it had read, the black dots between the spite-filled letters like bullet holes. Someone knew. My secret was no longer a secret.

'What do you think, Mallow?'

'Huh?' Both the doctor and Mum were staring at me.

'Oh, for goodness' sake, Mallow,' said Mum, frowning. 'Doctor, I'm sure you understand what a big thing this is for a teenager to have to put up with. Fifteen months; that's how long this has been going on. There must be something else we can try. What about hair cell cloning or that new pill they're using in the US?'

I gazed at Mum. Every evening she sat at the kitchen table, glued to her laptop – she was turning into a walking medical encyclopaedia.

'We're a long way from that being an alternative here,' said Dr Violetta, tapping at her keyboard. 'I understand this must be frustrating, but we're doing all we can. Mallow, you're seeing the dermatologist again in six months, so let's see what she says.'

'We were hoping for an appointment before then,

weren't we, Mallow?' Mum grabbed her bag and stood up.

'I guess,' I said.

Dr Violetta removed her glasses and pressed the skin under her eyes. 'It's a question of waiting lists.' She swivelled her chair to face me. 'In my opinion your scalp might benefit from having a rest from treatments, anyway.'

As we drove to pick Cal up from his friend's, I itched to tell Mum about the message. But that nerve in her jaw was twitching, and her knuckles had turned stripy red and white from clenching the steering wheel.

'There has to be something out there somewhere. Don't worry, love, we won't give up,' she said, staring grimly through the windscreen. 'Even if we have to get you to the States.'

'Can we afford it?'

'We'll think of something. I'll talk to your dad when he's next home.'

Going to the US seemed as likely as flying to Jupiter. It would cost way more than Mum and Dad could afford. They'd already forked out thousands on my wigs made from real hair. And what would happen to Gran? One of the reasons we'd moved into Gran's house was so Mum could look after her when she got out of hospital. She wouldn't want to stick her own mum in a nursing home, even if it was only temporary. And Bilbo would hate being in kennels for weeks. If only Dad were at home. Sometimes he was easier to talk to than stressy Mum, who was always 'busy, busy, busy' sorting out this, or making plans for that. But Dad was miles away. On an oil rig. In the North Sea. The Middle of Nowhere. He couldn't get further away if he tried.

Mum started nattering on about Gran's pneumonia (she was super-ill this time), and Cal's new photography club (he was doing *so* well). I rubbed a sleeve over the steamed-up side window. It had rained since we'd been in the surgery and dark blobby clouds were still over the town. The wet tarmac glowed orange from the streetlights. We turned into the blustery promenade. A wide strip of paving hugged the shingle beach on one side and the main road ran along the other. At the end was the crazy golf course and a metal sculpture. It was supposed to look like the Eiffel Tower but I thought it was more like a mini electricity pylon. *Very* classy. There were wooden panels around the tower, which stood on a concrete platform jutting onto the beach. When the tide came in, the tower was surrounded by water on three sides. When there was a gale, it creaked and whistled.

The rush hour traffic had slowed to a crawl. A couple

of gulls screeched overhead. Now and then a car whooshed by in the opposite lane, spraying puddle-water in all directions. As we inched past the statue of a man looking out to sea – I could never remember his name – a movement flickered at the corner of my eye. I twisted round. As usual, an orange traffic cone was on the statue's head. But there was something else. A dark, hooded shape with a backpack crouched at the base of the statue, as if tying a loose shoelace. Something in the way he checked around himself made me stare harder, but the rain on the window obscured my view. As the car finally began to move faster, the figure blurred and disappeared.

Chapter Two

It was meant to be a fresh start, moving to Framton-on-Sea. A chance to forget Sara and my other 'mates' who'd mutated into enemies. To have no more in-my-face reminders of *that* day (though I'd never forget it). A new home where my secret would stay a secret, and I'd have a sparkly new life with real friends. Where people would meet the new me – the one with hair.

It *had* been going well.

'Are you even listening?' said Trude, stopping so suddenly I cannoned into her.

'Course.'

'What did I just say then?'

'Uh . . .'

'I knew it! You haven't heard a word.'

'Sorry,' I murmured. 'What was it?'

'I was talking ideas,' said Trude. 'For our business. Have you got any? My cousin makes jewellery out of felt . . . we don't have to do that but . . .' She broke off. 'Oh hun, you're not looking at that message again? I told you to delete it.' She propelled me to a nearby bench which faced the beach, wrestled the phone from my fingers and peered at the tiny cracked screen. 'There's no point staring at it all the time.'

'But someone *knows*.' The words came out in a whisper.

'It's just some idiot playing a sick joke.' Her arm circled my shoulders and squeezed. 'So what if people find out, they'll forget quickly. Nobody will care. You can't help having alopecia. And look at the celebs who are bald. There's that TV presenter and the Olympic cyclist for starters . . .' Trude looked at me. 'If it were me, I wouldn't care what other people thought.'

'But I'm not you,' I said, shrugging her arm away. 'I want people to stare at me for having the bluest eyes or the brightest smile, not the shiniest scalp.'

I knew she was only trying to cheer me up. Funny, warm-hearted Trude, who I'd played with since I was small, whenever we'd visited Gran in Framton. Who'd looked after me since we'd moved here from London three months ago and I'd started at Framton Academy. Who'd been my friend *before* my hair fell out and was becoming a better mate every day. Even she didn't understand what it was like to be different, to have people call you 'Baldilocks' and 'Marshmallow Head', to have them gape, touch, tug and . . . My thoughts flitted back again to my old school. Cringe-filled memories. Arriving home, seeing the police car outside the house, Mum and Dad's faces, my promise to 'never do it again' . . . *Shudder*.

I seized the phone back from Trude, tapped the screen and waited while it connected to the unfamiliar number, trying not to worry about what I'd say if someone answered. An automated voice told me to leave a message. I hit 'End Call' and rammed the phone deep into my school bag.

'You're not gonna want to hear this,' said Trude, getting to her feet. 'But you won't be able to keep your alopecia a secret forever. Especially when this creep posts about it on Chat-Scape. You're lucky they haven't done it already.'

'You're right.' I sighed. Gossip spread like crazy on Chat-Scape. The creep was sure to spill the beans sooner or later.

Once we reached the high wall outside school, we started to dawdle. Trude brought a mirror out to gloss her lips while I fiddled with my fringe. You wouldn't imagine Trude and I had anything in common. Perfect skin; deep blue eyes; long legs; blonde, swishy hair – that was Trude. Dumpy; murky, grey-blue eyes; a huge pimple on the chin – that was me. I did have great hair, it just wasn't mine.

As my heart gave a sickening kick at the thought of the day ahead, Trude linked my arm. 'Safety in numbers,' she said with a shiny smile. 'We'll fight this together. You can be Robina to my Wigwoman.'

'Hey, I'm the one with the wig.' I couldn't help grinning. Trude always managed to cheer me up.

'Get lost. It's my idea.'

'So where are our capes?'

'Hmm, good point.' Trude thought for a moment. 'We'll have to be Blazer Battlers. Our special power can be . . .' She pressed a finger to her chin and scrunched her eyebrows together. 'Supersonic speed. And we'll fight crime, injustice and bald-ism wherever we find it. Nobody will dare stand in our way.'

'We need a motto,' I said. 'Like Boldly Battling for Baldness or something.'

We were still chuckling as we entered the school gates.

Chapter Three

Gaggles of tiny Year Sevens were huddled by the railings; other people milled around in little gangs, including some boys from our tutor group. Fraser and Archie were there, sniggering at something on Fraser's phone. *Please don't let it be about me.* Dan from my maths class was leaning against the wall next to the water fountain, hands stuffed into his pockets, looking at the ground. Everything appeared normal, but a shiver still scuttled down my spine. The creep could be right there, watching, waiting . . .

'I'm going to the canteen.' I was feeling jumpy again.

'Get me a bacon bap, will you?' said Trude as she ran to join Fraser and Archie.

As I rummaged in my bag for my purse, pages from my history file burst out and fluttered to the ground. I crouched to pick them up, praying my homework wasn't trashed.

'Here.' A shadow fell across the ground where I knelt and the next thing I knew Dan was squatting beside me, a fistful of papers in his hand. As he tossed his floppy hair back, I caught sight of his chocolate eyes. He held out the sheets and my heart swooped.

Trude said Dan was weird because he was stand-offish and never talked much. But I reckoned he only spoke when he had something worth saying. I thought that was cool.

'Hope they're not ruined.'

'Don't think so.' My cheeks were burning.

We both chose that instant to stand up. Our heads cracked together.

'My fault,' said Dan, rubbing his forehead. 'You okay?'

'I think . . .' My hand flew up to smooth my wig.

'Chill, your head's still there.' Dan was staring at me, his head tilted. He had a quirky smile – kind of turned up on one side and down on the other.

I whipped my hand behind my back so he couldn't see how much it was trembling. 'Oh, right.' My laugh was *so* forced.

'Hi, Mallow. Hi, Dan.' It was Faye 'I-was-friends-with-Trude-long-before-you-came-along' Turner. She was with Em.

I battled to stuff the grubby papers back in my file. Dan nodded at the two of them and moved off, leaving us to stare after him.

'You've got to admit he's cute,' said Faye.

'No way. He's weird. Can't think what you see in him,' said Em. She sucked at a strand of her hair as we watched him disappear around the corner of the sports hall. 'What did he want with *you*, Mallow?'

'Nothing.'

Em arched her eyebrows, making her steely eyes grow large. '*Really?* Come on, spill. He must have said something.'

They were both staring at me now. Faye's glare was razor-sharp. My cheeks flamed again. 'He didn't get the chance.' All because Em and Faye had arrived. Why did they choose today to butt in? The one day when Dan had decided to speak to me properly, rather than mutter 'Hi,' as we passed in the corridor.

Faye gave a little cough. 'We were chatting, me and Em.' She tucked a coppery curl behind one ear and gazed at me, her hazel eyes magnified by owlish glasses. 'Do you want to come for a sleepover one weekend?'

'What?' I swallowed hard. My thoughts were no longer

on Dan.

'You know, that thing where you go to someone's house and stay the night,' said Faye, rolling her eyes. 'Or didn't you do that with your old mates?'

Alarm bells were clanging in my head. I didn't know what to say. Why were they asking me now? Em and I had started at the same time at Framton Academy, but we'd never got on. In fact, she'd gone out of her way to ignore me. And Faye had had plenty of sleepovers with Trude and Em, and never ONCE invited me. Not that it bothered me (much) because sleepovers were Number One on my THINGS NOT TO DO list.

'We could go into town first. There's that boutique on the High Street,' continued Faye. 'It's got some brilliant tops.'

Tappity-bang, tappity-bang. The sound of the final nail being hammered into my coffin. Number Two on my list. Shopping trips were pure STRESS. What if my wig got tangled on a button or something? Or Faye and Em wanted to try out HAIR STUFF? So many chances for them to notice my wig.

'Weekends are pretty busy for me.' I felt a twang of shame at the lie.

'If you don't want to hang around with us you just have

to say,' said Faye.

'I didn't mean—'

'Yeah, we're obviously not as exciting as your *London* friends,' said Em, sniffing.

'No,' I squeaked. 'Of course I want to . . .' Another whopper. On the one hand Faye and Em gave me the jitters – they didn't know me like Trude did – on the other, they were trying to be friendly, *weren't they*? And that had to be a good thing. I could almost hear the seconds ticking by as they waited for me to speak.

'A Saturday might work,' I said at last.

Faye exchanged glances with Em. 'Okay, I'll ask my mum about dates and stuff.' Em grabbed Faye's arm and pulled her away, whispering in her ear. Then Em looked back at me and smirked before they disappeared in the same direction as Dan.

I let out a breath. I'd have to pray Faye would forget the invitation, but knowing my luck that was as likely as my hair growing back overnight.

A bleep from the depths of my bag. *Ignore it*, my brain urged, but not before the phone lay hot and heavy in my hand. If someone was trying to freak me out, they were doing a good job.

A message from the same number.

Find the wig and keep your secret.

Chapter Four

'Mum, it doesn't fit!' I lobbed the wig across my room towards the bin. 'It's scratchy and hot. I hate it.'

After twenty HIDEOUS minutes of morning wig-fixing, a messy lump of hair was now drooped over the waste bin like a floppy, blonde spider. I slumped onto the bed, crushing my school uniform, and buried my head in my hands. There was a creak of floorboards and the lumpy mattress sank as Mum sat next to me.

'I . . . *can't* go to school!' I wailed, swiping at the snot dribbling from my nose. Bilbo's warm dog breath tickled my face; I pushed him away. 'Everyone will find out.' *If they don't already know*, screamed the voice inside my head.

'The wig is the same as yesterday. Nothing's changed.

I promise, nobody will notice.'

Mum pulled me towards her like she always did when I had a wobbly wig moment. Familiar flowery perfume wafted from her jumper as I snuffled and sniffed and sagged against her. She pressed her soft lips against the top of my scalp. 'I'll help fix your wig. Wash your face first and we'll get cracking.'

'I'm a freak.' My breath hiccoughed.

'You're not a freak. You're fabulous.'

'All right, I'm a fabulous freak,' I said with a shaky giggle.

'*My* fabulous freak,' said Mum, pulling away and cupping my soggy cheeks in her palms.

I wiped my eyes and gave a faltering smile. There were so many reasons to stay off school, all jostling for first place in my brain. In London, Mum let me stay at home on Bad Hair Days – when I was still getting used to my wig, worried that the slightest draught would whisk it off, or when I couldn't cope with the whispers. Mum would take the day off work too, if Dad was on the rig, and we'd snuggle under my duvet and watch black and white movies. But that wasn't going to happen this time because I hadn't told Mum about the messages.

That second one had freaked me out. Who had sent it?

What did it mean? Did everyone know about my hair? What if, what if . . . ? I hadn't dared check my phone or log on to Chat-Scape yet this morning, I was so petrified of what I might find. But Mum seemed calmer today. I snuggled up to her again. Maybe now would be the time to mention the messages.

'I get that you don't like wearing your wig,' said Mum, before I'd opened my mouth. 'Have you given any more thought to—?'

'No way.' I prised my head away from her jumper. 'I'm not going in without it.'

'What happened before won't happen again, love.'

'You don't know that,' I said, looking at her through blurry eyes.

'Well, Miss Reach said if you decided—'

'Mum, there's something I need—'

A sudden crash came from downstairs, followed by a yell. Bilbo barked.

'What on earth?' Mum pulled away. 'Must be that brother of yours dropping things again. I'd better sort it out.'

Something clattered up the stairs, then Cal's head peeped round the door. 'Mum, the dishwasher's kind of busted. It wasn't my fault. Honest.'

'As if I didn't have enough to deal with.' Mum sighed. 'Coming now.'

Cal threw the door wide open. He still had his pyjamas on. His bony knee was poking through a hole in the trouser bottoms.

'Has someone died?' he said, looking first at me, then Mum. I glared at him.

'No,' said Mum. 'Nothing to concern you, Cal.'

'Oh, I get it,' he said. 'It's a wig thing.'

'Out!' I yelled. The pillow missed Cal's head by millimetres.

Mum planted a kiss on my forehead and glanced at her watch. 'When you're ready, I'll help with your hair, then I've got to go shopping before I see Gran. Let's hope there's better news from the hospital. It's all been so worrying. I'll send her your love, shall I?' I nodded. She gave a tired smile and got to her feet. 'Oh, what did you want to say, love?'

'It's not important.'

'Sure?' Mum turned away and headed for the door, Bilbo at her heels.

'Yep.'

Clunk. The door shut.

I pressed a hand on the warm spot on the bed. I'd

missed my chance.

In the end, I fixed the wig on my own – Mum was too busy clearing up the mess in the kitchen – and twenty minutes later I was trudging down Gran's long driveway to meet Trude.

'Didn't you get my message?' said Trude as soon as I got close enough to hear.

'Sorry, no.'

'I've been waiting ages.' She looked at me. 'Bad Hair Day?'

'Yep.'

She gave a sympathetic grunt. 'I guess you haven't been on Chat-Scape this morning either? There's no mention of you. That's good, isn't it?'

I shrugged.

When I didn't say anything, Trude pulled out her phone. 'Check this out. I've subscribed to the Young Entrepreneur app. They've got loads of stuff about starting a business. It could be handy. What do you think?'

I glanced at the screen, but I couldn't get excited about Trude's plan. Why was the message creep keeping quiet on Chat-Scape? Something didn't add up. If you had a secret this MASSIVE, you'd blab to everyone, wouldn't you?

*

'Stay behind please, Mallow,' said Miss Reach as we packed up after English, the last lesson of the day.

The others filed out the classroom while I watched in silence, wishing I were one of them.

'Take a seat.' Miss Reach gestured at the chair next to her desk and shooed the stragglers from the room.

The door snapped shut. Miss Reach had her serious tutor face on, the one where she pressed her lips together so tightly they practically disappeared. What if she'd noticed me checking my mobile all afternoon? Maybe she'd somehow heard about the messages. My phone dug into my palm as I sat on the edge of the seat.

Miss Reach peered at me. 'How are you getting on? I hope you're settling in okay?'

I nodded.

'You're happy here?'

I nodded again.

Please don't mention my alopecia.

'And any problems managing your alopecia here at school?'

Groan.

'No,' I mumbled.

'The students are generally a friendly bunch, as I'm

sure you've found. But if you've got any worries or if anyone's giving you a hard time, we can sort it out.' Miss Reach's eyes creased at the corners. 'I realise you don't want people to find out about your hair loss, but sometimes it's harder to keep a secret than to let it out.'

I blushed and Miss Reach gave me a concerned look. When I kept quiet, she sighed and flicked through one of the books on her desk as if looking for something.

'A group has just been started, for students who might want a safe place to meet and talk. It's lead by our school counsellor, Mrs Jacobi.' Miss Reach slid an A4 sheet across her desk. 'Monday lunchtimes in B6, if you're interested.'

I didn't say anything, but picked up the paper and stuffed it in my pocket.

'Remember, Mallow, if you want to chat you can come and see me anytime. And I mean that: anytime.' She paused. 'There's nothing you want to talk about right now?'

'No, I'm fine.'

'Okay. You're doing excellent work in English at the moment.' Her piercing gaze swung between her pile of books and the mobile in my hand. 'The next couple of years are important ones. You won't get distracted, will you?'

'No.' I swallowed, hard. 'Thanks.'

At last she let me go, and I trailed down the corridor, phone clutched tight, determined to get rid of the nasty messages. I'd try to forget about them and hope whoever was responsible would leave me alone. My thumb hovered over 'Delete', but at that moment the mobile bleeped. I stopped dead. With legs like jelly, I leant against the wall. The corridor was deserted, but there was a faint chatter coming from the staff lounge. Everyone else must have either gone home or outside.

My willpower to ignore the messages drained away as quickly as it'd come. Robot-like, I tapped the message icon. An image of the seafront flashed up, a queue of cars on the far side of the road, the beams from their headlamps splintering on the wet tarmac. The sky was leaden and the paving slabs of the prom looked slippery. I spied the fuzzy outline of the statue with a blurry red splodge beside its grey base. Nothing unusual. Except . . . my throat constricted.

There was no orange traffic cone on the head of the statue. Instead, something else sat on the top of it.

It couldn't be . . . I squinted at the image, trying to make sense of it.

Too small for the statue's head, the wig had slipped

sideways and was dangling like a limp rag. Damp tendrils of long, blonde-ish hair spread out over the sides of the face. A wig chosen to look like mine. To anyone else it would have seemed hilarious. Not to me.

Heat prickled across my scalp. I took a deep breath and tapped in:

Who are you?

For a second I stared at the words, then I hit delete. What was the point? As if this person would tell me. I thought of Miss Reach and her words: 'come and see me anytime'. I took two paces back towards her door and froze. Mr Das Gupta had appeared outside the classroom.

'Still here, Mallow?'

'Yes, sir,' I squeaked.

'Everything all right?' His gaze drilled into mine.

'Yes, sir.' *Say something*, I willed myself. But the words refused to come, stuck somewhere between my tonsils and lips.

His eyebrows rose a fraction higher. 'Something wrong? Need help with the homework? Some of those quadratic equations are difficult.'

'No, everything's good,' I uttered at last, and gave a half-smile.

Mr Das Gupta was already turning away. 'Time you

went home then.'

Miss Reach's door shut with a clunk. My thoughts zigzagged as I stared at the two blurry figures through the frosted glass window. If I told Miss Reach what was going on, she'd investigate. But then people would definitely find out about my hair. She'd discuss it with other teachers. All the attention would be on me – people would stare and whisper. Just like in London. But if I kept quiet, where would this end? Wouldn't people find out anyway?

What I was about to do was A BAD IDEA. Even so, I dashed out of the main school building, twisted between the canteen and sports hall, pelted across the car park and along East End Road. The muscles in my legs burnt as I hurtled along the pavement, tearing past a surprised Trude and Faye, and only slowing as I reached the statue.

Blood pounded in my ears as I came to a halt. I leant over for a moment, hands on knees, fighting for air. Finally, I struggled upright and glanced left to right along the prom. A few people scuttled past, walking dogs or on their way home from work, but no one was looking in my direction. At the top of the statue perched a lonely gull, pecking at the bronze. No wig. I searched the ground around the base of the statue, assuming it had slipped off. There was no sign of it.

Trude arrived.

'What's going on?' she panted.

Numbly, I handed her my phone.

'This is not funny, hun,' she said, enveloping me in a hug, her breath tickling my cheek. 'Let's go home and tell your mum. Get her to sort it out with school.'

I wished it were that simple. Mum and Dad always told me not to leave little worries bottled up inside until they grew too big. But this worry was already huge and, with Mum getting super-stressy about Gran being so sick with pneumonia, she'd explode if I gave her more problems. An image popped into my mind of 'forever-the-lawyer' Mum storming up to see the head, threatening a legal suit against the culprit. And then me – friendless, alone, my classmates calling me 'Baldie Blabbermouth' and snickering behind my back. The brand-new life I'd built for myself in Framton would be over before it had hardly begun.

For a moment I contemplated snatching the phone from Trude, hurling it into the scummy sea and watching it smash into tiny fragments against the pebbles. But what difference would it make? I had a nasty feeling this creep would get to me another way.

'What's up, Mallow?' Faye was standing at the base of the statue, staring at me.

'Nothing,' I said, trying to compose my face.

'Just a stupid joke,' said Trude. 'Someone being nasty. Come on, let's go.' She marched off up the road. I moved to follow her.

'Mallow,' said Faye, putting out a hand to stop me.

'Yeah?' I twisted round to face her.

Faye hesitated, kicking at the uneven paving slabs with the toe of her shoe. I waited for her to speak. Finally she said, 'See you around.'

I shrugged, too shaken up to worry about Faye, and hurried after Trude.

'I don't want to tell Mum. Not yet, anyway,' I said as soon as I'd caught up with her. My voice came out shaky. 'I can sort this out myself . . . somehow.'

'You're not alone,' said Trude. 'We're in this together. Remember, we're Wigwoman and Robina!'

I squeezed her hand. Even though we'd only been 'proper' mates for a few months it was as if Trude knew me inside out. Without her, my life would have been pretty unbearable. But that fact didn't stop the fear that sizzled from my scalp to my toes.

Chapter Five

After saying a glum goodbye to Trude at Gran's gate, I headed down the twisty driveway towards the house. Thick branches stretched in a high arch above me, blocking out the wintry sunlight. My arms tingled with goosebumps as leaves rustled around. I stole a glance behind, convinced someone was watching. *Relax*, I told myself. *There's no one there.*

I trudged round the back of Gran's house, into the courtyard, giving the green wheelie bin a kick as I passed. Someone had it in for me. There had to be a way to find out who was sending the messages. I just needed time to think . . .

I spotted Mr Grainger. He and his wife lived in the converted stable block next door. He was standing – as he always did at this time of day – at the kitchen sink. He flapped a yellow rubber-gloved hand, calling out through the open window, 'Gran still in hospital, Mallow?'

I gave a quick wave and continued through the courtyard. Most afternoons I'd stop for a chat, but not today. My head was filled with a vision of the wig-wearing statue shouting, 'Freak!' and, 'Baldie!' as it strode along the prom.

No one was around when I went into the kitchen to fill a hot-water bottle. Thanks to the dodgy heating system and draughty nooks, the Old Vicarage was always like a freezer. I didn't know how Gran could stand it, but she said she had iron for bones and didn't feel the cold. The iron wasn't working too well though now, I thought, remembering how fragile she'd looked on my last visit to see her in hospital. I headed for the box room, a tiny space at the back of the house that was sandwiched between the bathroom and Cal's bedroom. This was where Gran's ancient computer was. Mum's laptop would have been better but it wasn't in its usual spot on the kitchen worktop and I couldn't be bothered to hunt around for it. Besides, Mum didn't like me using it while she was doing her 'research', or whatever it was she did on it. As there was no heater in the box room I wrapped myself in a blanket from the airing cupboard, stuffed the hot-water bottle up my jumper and borrowed Cal's fingerless gloves.

My phone bleeped while I was waiting for the computer to boot up. Only Trude.

You OK, hun?

Yeah, I'm fine, I replied and pocketed my phone. Finally, the computer sprang to life and I logged into the Chat-Scape site. My fingers were near-frozen but my scalp tingled hot as I scrolled through all the recent messages and photos, convinced at any moment I'd come across one labelled 'BALDIE'. There were loads posted by Beth from my tutor group and Archie with jokey comments underneath. Some by Faye. Fraser had posted a video of him playing Crusade, and suddenly his voice was booming around the room. I frantically clicked the mouse to mute it, muttering under my breath. The good thing was there was nothing posted about me. Yet.

I shut my eyes for a moment and took a few deep breaths, willing my heart rate to slow. In . . . out . . . in . . . out. Perhaps focusing on my homework would help me forget what had happened. I opened my geography document on volcanic eruptions. A snag of nail hung off my little finger and I nibbled it as I stared at the half-finished work. I hadn't told anyone about my alopecia and I was convinced Trude hadn't either. I trusted her with my life. Dad was hardly around, so that left Mum and Cal. Maybe one of them had let something slip by mistake . . .

'Mallow,' called Mum. 'I'm home!'

I slouched downstairs into the kitchen. Bilbo was bouncing around Mum's legs. When he saw me, he leapt up in mad spaniel excitement.

'He dragged me for miles today. I'm wrecked.' Mum sounded cross, but I knew she didn't mean it. She wouldn't be without him. 'Can you lay the table, love?'

'Off, boy!' I pushed his muddy paws from my skirt and bent to tickle his golden ears. Then I set about digging knives and forks out of the cutlery drawer and filling glasses with water. 'Mum, have you mentioned *it* to anyone?'

'What do you mean?' asked Mum, frowning as she pulled off her coat. She *knew* what I meant. 'Has something happened?'

'Course not,' I lied hurriedly. Mum had tensed up like a coiled spring. 'It was just . . . someone told a hair joke at school today. It wasn't even said to me.'

'Probably nothing then,' said Mum, her shoulders relaxing slightly. 'Perhaps I should ring Miss Reach anyway and have a chat to her.'

'It's nothing, Mum. Please don't.' The last thing I wanted was control-freak Mum bulldozing her way into school, swooping in to sort out the problem, and making things worse for me.

'I want to help, love. After what happened last time . . .' A muscle in her jaw twitched.

'Please, Mum.'

She hesitated. 'Okay, we'll leave things for now and see how they go.'

That sounded vague.

'But promise you'll tell me if there's the first hint of any trouble?' she continued. 'Best to nip these things in the bud.'

'Promise,' I said, crossing my fingers behind my back. 'What time is Dad calling?'

'Should be soon,' said Mum, glancing at the clock. 'By the way, I've got something for you. Came in today's post.'

'Early Christmas present?' I joked. My heart flipped. Maybe she'd bought me a mobile to replace my lousy old one. I'd been going on about it for ages. When everything was settled with the move, Mum and Dad had said. The timing couldn't have been better. A new phone meant a different number which nobody would know. There'd be no more horrid messages. I'd make sure I only gave my new number to the people I trusted. AND I'd be able to play games on it.

'Take a look,' said Mum, turning to fill the sink with water. 'I put it in the dresser to keep it safe. Top drawer.'

I pulled open the drawer. At the front, nestled between the place mats and yellowing paper napkins, was a white cardboard box the same size and shape as a toothpaste carton. *That can't be it*, I thought and dug deeper, hoping to find something more phone-sized. After more pointless rummaging, I gave up and lifted out the carton.

'I sent off for it last week,' said Mum. She rubbed her hands on a tea towel and came over. 'It arrived quicker than I thought.'

'What is it?' I asked, though I'd already guessed. The word 'Replenish' was emblazoned on the carton in dazzling fluorescent green.

'Just apply it twice a day. It's supposed to help stimulate the hair follicles,' said Mum, her voice high and chirpy.

'Mum—'

'I know, I know, the doctor said to give your scalp a rest,' she continued. 'But you want to carry on trying things, don't you? And this has got good reviews. Look.'

She pulled her reading glasses from her handbag and sat at the laptop. She brought up a website and read out a load of medical promotional stuff.

She pushed her glasses onto her head and looked at me. 'I've done the research, been online and found loads of people who've tried it. Their hair started growing back within days and with no side effects. You never know, this could be the one! Better than waiting to see what the consultant says in six months.' She reached out a hand and squeezed my arm. 'What about trying it now, love?'

I shrugged.

'A bit of enthusiasm wouldn't go amiss,' said Mum.

'I've tried loads of things and none of them have worked.'

'It might be different with this.'

'Fine, but it'll be your fault if I come out in a hideous rash like that other time.' I seized the carton and flounced from the room.

'Don't be like that, love,' called Mum as I thumped up the stairs.

So this was the 'research' Mum had mentioned. It had been months since I'd last logged on to the support sites, even longer since I'd posted anything myself. But Mum was always ready to try the next thing. The setbacks didn't seem to affect her like they did me. That would be because she wasn't the one massaging gloop on her head.

In the bathroom, I pulled off my wig and scrunched up my eyes before turning towards the mirror above the basin. This was the bit I hated. I took a deep breath, opened one eyelid and squinted at my reflection, hoping that somehow my head wouldn't look as bad as the last time I'd checked. No such luck. I twisted one way, then the other. My hair used to be blonde and thick, falling below my shoulders in a choppy style. Most of the time I'd worn it loose or plaited the strands at the sides of my face. It had looked pretty cool. The fringe had swept over to the side, almost covering one eye.

I'd been staring in the mirror just like this when I'd found the first bald patch. Correction: it had been Sara who'd found it. We were in the toilets during lunchtime, standing in front of the row of basins. She'd been fiddling with my hair. We were giggling, messing about, trying to recreate the 1960s beehive style Sara had seen in *Vogue* – she was into things like that. I remembered the sudden silence, and her horrified face reflected in the mirror.

'Mallow, you're going bald!' she'd shrieked, teasing the strands apart to get a better look. 'There's a huge bald patch right here!'

34

Jess and Tabitha and Lorna had crowded round to gawp, gasping and screeching, 'Gross!' and, 'Don't touch it, she might be contagious.' They'd got their phones out and taken photos, cackling as they shared them around. I still remembered my fingertips seeking the spot at the back of my head, as big as a fifty pence, and touching the smooth, soft skin of my scalp for the first time. A wave of sickness swamped me.

Now what remained of my hair was a disaster. Between the acres of shiny scalp covered in spidery veins, blonde wisps floated at right angles to my head. Thicker tufts stuck out over the tops of my ears and down the sides of my scalp. I leant against the basin to examine my brows and lashes in the mirror. Still there, thank goodness. Without them my face would disappear.

I opened the carton, skimmed the instructions and squirted a greasy blob on my finger. Then I rubbed it in with small, circular motions, the formula tingling my skin. As soon as I finished, I inspected my head, searching for the first fuzz of regrown hair. As if the cream would have worked straightaway. Obviously, there was nothing. Nada. Zilch. Zip. I placed the tube on the shelf and glanced at my reflection in the mirror, making my usual wish to the 'hair fairy' or whoever was up there:

Please, please, please let my hair grow back.

The phone trilled from the hall.

'Got it!' I yelled, sprinting onto the landing and down the stairs.

'Hello?' Dad's voice crackled and buzzed over the wobbly connection. 'How's tricks, poppet?' My heart lifted – so much had happened in the last few days, it seemed like years since I'd seen him, even though it was really only three weeks.

'You've got to rescue me,' I grumped before I could stop myself. 'Gran's house is as cold as an igloo and I'm sure my big toe's got frostbite.' That wasn't what I'd planned to say. I'd *planned* to tell Dad about the creepy messages, the photo on my phone and the wig on the statue – about how scared I was – but the distance between us down the muffled line stretched too far. And even if I did say something, what could he do from the middle of the North Sea?

'Tell you what, I'll bring a polar bear skin back with me,' he was saying. 'There's one around here somewhere. That'll keep you roasty-toasty at night.'

'Not funny,' I said, remembering my beautiful, carved white bed back in London, with its comfy mattress, thick duvet and fluffy pillows. 'It's all right for you – you're not here most of the time. Can't we move into our own place?'

'Hang in there. It'll be fantastic in a few months, you'll see. Think of the long, sunny days in the garden. And the beach will be great.'

'Okay,' I said, though I found it hard to imagine Framton-on-Sea ever being warm and summery. 'Wish you were here though.'

'Wish I were there too,' he said, his voice going croaky. He coughed. 'Anyway, that's why I'm ringing. I'll be home the day after tomorrow. Two whole weeks of me and you'll be begging me to leave again.' I giggled but we both knew I missed him loads when he went away. It was tricky having a part-time dad who only saw a tiny bit of my life when he came home from the rig. It'd been super hard when I'd lost my hair and he'd set eyes on my patchwork scalp for the first time. He hadn't known what to say, but I'd spotted tears as he gathered me in his huge arms and hugged me tight, as if he'd never let me go.

'Can't wait to see you,' I said.

'Ditto.' There was a pause. 'How's Gran?'

'Mum thinks she's getting better and will be home soon.'

'Good news,' said Dad. 'Take care of your mum, Mallow. She's got a lot on her plate, what with looking after Gran and the move. Hold things together till I get back – can you do that for me?'

All I could manage was a snuffle.

'Are you still there?'

'Uh-huh.'

'I've only got a few more minutes,' said Dad. 'Phil's off sick and I'm having to cover his work . . . But is everything okay? No problems at school I should know about?'

'I'm fine,' I said, managing to speak properly at last. How could I squeeze in what I wanted to say with the clock ticking?

'Okay, poppet. Well, remember to get the banner out.' Dad's standing joke. But Cal and I hadn't put up the 'Welcome Home, Dad!' sign in ages; the novelty of him boomeranging back and forth wore off a long time ago.

'Better pass me over to Mum, so I can have a quick word,' he said. 'I'll see you Saturday.'

'Great!' I said. It would be better seeing him face-to-face – I'd collar him on his own, without Mum there to make things stressy, and spill the beans. That thought made me feel happier. I would tell him EVERYTHING. He'd know what to do.

Chapter Six

Saturday. Through the kitchen window I watched the pale sun peep out from behind wispy white clouds. Mum's idea of a picnic on the strip of stones people called the beach didn't seem as insane as it had earlier in the week. It was November and it was freezing but NOTHING could dent my happiness because Dad was coming home that afternoon. That wasn't even the best thing. The best thing was I'd had no more creepy messages or photos.

Mum wasn't visiting Gran today and Cal was buzzing around her like a wasp in a jam jar. She was in a rare good mood, chatting and laughing as she packed sandwiches, crisps and cake into a backpack.

'What else?' she said, half to herself, tapping a finger on her lips.

'The kite,' said Cal. He lobbed a tennis ball over my head and Bilbo chased it around the kitchen.

'Careful, ratbag,' I said, flicking Cal with a tea towel. He dodged it and I pulled the towel back for a second go, but he'd got hold of his own and now we were swiping at each other across the kitchen table.

'Strike!' yelled Cal, as he caught me on the arm.

'Not fair,' I said. 'I wasn't ready.' I managed a flick to his elbow before he darted out of the way.

'If you think you can beat the Tea Towel Terror, think again!' roared Cal. He leapt on a chair and twirled the towel around his head like a lasso.

I darted forwards and thwacked his calf as he launched himself off the chair and whipped me between the shoulder blades.

'Ouch!' I said, rubbing the sore spot. I chucked my tea towel on the table. 'Okay, okay, Tea Towel Terror. You win. Just wait till next time.'

Cal whooped, making Bilbo bark and run around in circles.

'You're acting like a pair of five year olds. I can't think with the racket you're making,' said Mum, but she was smiling.

'Yeah, Cal. Act your age, or they'll ban you from

starting Year Seven next year.' I smirked.

'You got in even though you're a DUMB BRAIN.'

'Enough, you two,' said Mum. 'Right, the food's sorted. Mallow, get the cricket stumps out.'

I always got the worst jobs – the old cricket set was in the understairs cupboard along with the coats, boots, Gran's battered Monopoly game and about a TRILLION spiders.

'Where's my camera?' said Cal as I returned holding the cricket set bag at arm's length to avoid the sticky cobwebs. 'I'm gonna take some cool shots today.'

'Good idea,' said Mum. 'Quite the photographer now, aren't you?'

'Can I print them out?'

'My printer's not up to the job. But I'll go to Happy Snaps when I'm next in town.'

'We're going to do outside shots at photography club next week,' said Cal.

My heart twanged as I listened to Mum and Cal's easy chatter, so different from the clashes she and I had been having lately. If only she'd talk to me about something other than doctors and treatments. If only one day we could go shopping for something other than a new wig.

'Have you asked if Trude wants to come?' said Mum.

I nodded. Trude had messaged to say she'd meet us on the beach.

The cold morning didn't bother us. We played with Bilbo, skimmed stones and watched Cal battle with his kite. After the picnic, Mum and Cal got busy with his camera. The last of the cotton-wool clouds scooted away, leaving a bright blue sky, and Trude and I lay on the rug, huddled in our coats. The wind had died down and we closed our eyes, enjoying the sunlight on our faces.

'Have you noticed the way Dan hangs around?' said Trude suddenly.

'What do you mean?' I asked, opening one eye and squinting at her.

'I think he likes you.'

'Get lost,' I said, nudging her with my elbow. 'He ignores me most of the time.'

'That's not how I see it,' said Trude, grinning at me.

'He probably hangs around cos he likes *you*.'

Trude snorted. 'Now that is ridiculous.'

'You think?'

'Hun, he's not my type. I'm into boys who actually talk.'

'Like Archie, you mean?'

Trude went pink. 'I wasn't thinking about anyone in

particular.'

I chuckled and rested my head on the rug. Dan *did* hang around a lot, but then so did Fraser and Archie. Did Dan like me? The thought gave me butterflies. There was something about the mysterious boy with the chocolate eyes . . .

'Hey, that Young Entrepreneur app is brilliant,' said Trude. 'It's got tons of info about starting a business. And it's got me thinking. Our business needs to be something unique. I've got a couple of ideas, but I need to talk to you about them—'

'I'll go with whatever you want.' I stretched my arms above my head and yawned. 'You decide.'

'Oh . . . but don't you want to know what my ideas are?' Trude sounded put out.

'I trust you to make the right choice,' I said as I twisted onto my side to face her. 'I mean, you're better at that kind of thing than me.'

'You do want to help me though, don't you?'

'Yeah, course. We'll get together after school next week and figure it all out, okay? Today, I just want to chill.' I turned onto my back again and gave a happy sigh. 'Wake me in an hour.'

'Uh-huh.'

BLEEP.

I sat up. My phone was on the rug next to me. A new message. I glanced up – Mum and Cal were playing cricket, giggling as Mum tried to catch the ball and tumbled onto the shingle. Neither of them were looking my way.

'Let's go for a walk,' said Trude. She dragged me to my feet.

'See you back home,' I called to Mum. She waved vaguely in my direction.

'What does it say?' Trude asked as soon as we were out of earshot.

I tapped on the icon, my insides flipping over.

This will drive you round the bend.

'That is seriously creepy,' said Trude, staring at the message.

'What does it mean?' A sudden eddy of wind scraped hair across my cheek. My stomach swirled. 'It doesn't make sense.'

Before we had a chance to say more there was another bleep. This time it was a picture. I clicked and we both stared. The little screen was filled with a close-up of the bulbous red nose and gaping mouth of a clown. Its thick crimson lips formed a menacing, toothless grin. The paint on the clown's face was chipped and flaking, revealing a scratched, grey surface underneath. I could just make out a tatty wig balancing on top of the clown's black hat.

'I know where this is,' said Trude suddenly. 'What's another way of saying "round the bend"?'

'Mad? Crazy?' I said, my mind racing.

'Exactly.'

'The Crazy Horse?' I said, remembering the pub where Mr Grainger went some days when Mrs Grainger was at the day centre.

'No, not there—' Trude stopped. She frowned.

'Where then? Let's go there now.' I tugged her arm.

'This is what they want you to do,' she said, staring at me intently. 'It's how they're getting their kicks. Remember what that other message said? "Find the wig and keep your secret." They're playing a horrible game.'

'I know, but sooner or later this creep is going to slip up,' I said. 'Then I'll catch them. There's no way I'm going to let them get away with it.'

Trude bit her lip. 'Okay, but I don't like it, hun. This whole thing is freaking me out.'

She wasn't the only one. 'What choices do I have? Ignore it and hope this creep will go away? Or find who's responsible and make them stop? I'd rather do something

45

than sit back and wait.'

At last she nodded and after a quick hug we set off across the shingle. Trude led the way as we raced along the prom, past the statue – I couldn't look at it now without imagining the wig on its head – and on towards the steel tower. As we pelted across the empty car park, the message suddenly made sense. The entrance to the crazy golf was right in front of us. In the breeze, a sign rattled against the wire fence. I vaguely remembered playing there with Trude when we were younger. One of the holes on the course was the clown in the photo.

Trude was examining the chain and padlock on the gate. 'I forgot it'd be closed for the winter.'

We peered through the wire. Overgrown bushes blocked most of the site from view and I couldn't see the clown. I knelt on the damp ground, searching for a gap to squeeze through. Trude joined me, pulling tufts of grass, weeds and thistles away from the bottom of the fence. After a minute, I stood up. Time was trickling away and with it my hope of discovering the message creep.

'I'm going over the top,' I said. My heart was thumping.

'What if someone comes?' said Trude.

'You keep guard. Shout out if you see anyone.' I lifted

a leg and placed the toe of my boot against the flimsy fence. The links cut into the sole. If I stretched, I could just touch the bar at the top. I gripped the wire loops with my fingers and tugged myself upwards. The further up I clambered, the more the fence bent and wobbled under my weight. By the time I reached the top, it was sagging so much I didn't so much vault as flop over. I thudded onto my back on the grass and lay there for a few seconds, trying to recover.

'Hurry up,' hissed Trude.

I lurched to my feet and gazed around the golf course. I scuttled past a plastic windmill and over a tiny bridge. Past holes one, two, three, four . . . A moment later I spotted the clown with its peeling paintwork. Even before I got close, I could see the wig wasn't there. It wasn't on the ground surrounding the hole either. I scanned the course, hoping to catch sight of a fleeing figure, but the place seemed deserted.

A loud crunch sounded nearby, like dry twigs snapping. I whipped my head around, squinting hard at the nearest bushes, trying to make out a human shape amongst the greenery. But there was nothing. Probably a squirrel, I told myself, ignoring the little voice in my head saying: *Since when did squirrels make so much noise?*

I took a few deep breaths to calm myself and turned back to the clown. The mouth formed the entrance for the golf ball, with a smaller exit hole at the back of its neck. I crouched to peer into the murkiness of the mouth, in case the wig had dropped inside or another clue had been left there. Total blackness greeted me, along with a damp, mouldy smell. I rolled my sleeve up and stuck my arm in up to the elbow. My fingers touched the gritty, damp ground and then found something long and flat. I grasped it between two fingers and pulled out an old lolly stick. Blank – not even one of the joke ones. I pocketed it and skirted round the clown, to the back. A couple of crushed drinks cans littered the ground, and a crumpled crisp packet poked out of the back of the clown's head. Nothing else. Trude shrieked. I hurried back towards the fence and saw her talking to a man wearing a grubby purple jumper and baseball cap. She'd manoeuvred herself so he faced away from the golf course and the fence.

'Only in the summer,' I heard the man say.

'Silly me, must have forgotten. Have you got a leaflet with the opening times? Then I won't forget again.'

The man mumbled something, and they headed off towards the old shack at the entrance to the course. Trude glanced back before they vanished around the corner. I heaved myself over the fence.

Not long after, Trude reappeared holding a crumpled leaflet. 'Find anything?'

I shook my head. 'Waste of time.'

We headed across the car park. As we reached the prom, I glanced back towards the crazy golf course. The fence still sagged in the middle where I'd gone over the top.

But it was something else which grabbed my attention.

I clutched at Trude's arm. A figure in a black hoodie was standing in front of the chain-link fence, beside a skateboard, holding what looked like a wig.

The person was staring in our direction, then set off at a sprint, leaving the board behind.

Trude and I raced back across the car park. By the time we reached the exit, the figure had disappeared.

Chapter Seven

I hurried back to where the figure had left the skateboard, and picked it up. The design on the surface was so worn away all that was left were purple and brown paint splodges, and the wood itself was scuffed and chipped at the edges. It looked as if it belonged on a rubbish tip. 'Why didn't they use the skateboard to get away?'

'Duh,' said Trude, pointing at the gravel. 'On *this*?'

I had to agree, but something about the abandoned board seemed off.

'Who'd go around on a skateboard as manky as this?' said Trude, scrunching her nose. 'It's pretty wrecked. I'm sure I've seen it somewhere.'

'Where?'

'I don't know. School, maybe.'

I looked doubtfully at the skateboard. It was hard to imagine anyone wanting to use such a dirty old thing.

We stopped off at the kiosk on the prom and Trude bought a cone of chips. I didn't want any; my stomach was churning. We sat on the wall looking out to the grey sea while Trude gobbled the chips and I tried to shoo away the gulls.

'Any ideas?' she said.

I shook my head. 'Loads of people have skateboards.'

'But not like that one,' she said, tapping her teeth with the wooden chip fork in thought.

I fished out my phone, and flipped between the images, as if they'd provide answers. Trude peered at the grainy photo of the statue then pointed at the shiny paving slabs. 'The pavement's wet in this one.'

I cast my mind back, trying to remember when it had last rained. It came in a flash. Tuesday. It had rained on and off for most of the day. Mum and I had been to the doctor's, and we'd driven back along the prom, past the statue. I jolted as I remembered the figure huddled at its base. I mentioned it to Trude.

'Do you reckon it could be the same person?' Trude asked, nibbling on another chip.

I shrugged. 'I wish I'd been able to see more.'

'Don't worry – we'll sort it.' She was silent for a minute as she scrunched her chip cone into a ball and lobbed it at the nearby bin. It missed. With a sigh I got to my feet and went to pick it up. Further along the prom I could see a figure walking towards the railway bridge. It was Dan.

Trude was staring in that direction too. 'Wow—' She broke off, her face going pale.

I sat back down beside her on the bench. 'What is it?'

'Don't bite my head off, hun, but I've seen Dan with a board.'

'That Dan?' I said, pointing at him in the distance, just about to disappear under the bridge.

'We don't know any other Dans, do we?'

My heart dipped. Quiet, loner Dan was the last person I'd have imagined being involved in this.

'I know,' said Trude, clocking the doubt on my face. 'But I'm sure his is like this one – he uses it to get to school sometimes.'

'It can't be him,' I said, remembering him rescuing my homework at school, and his cute, lop-sided grin.

'But it makes sense,' said Trude. 'He *is* a bit odd. And he keeps himself to himself. Even Archie and Fraser don't know anything about him, and they're supposed to be his mates.'

'But you said he hangs around cos he likes me . . .'

'Maybe I was wrong about that, hun. Maybe he hangs around for a different reason. He could have been the one at the crazy golf. When he saw us, he panicked.'

'But why would he ditch his board?' The idea that Dan was responsible for the messages made my stomach heave. 'It's like leaving a big sign saying "It was me."'

'He might have just forgotten it, you know, in a panic?'

'But he wouldn't still be hanging around here, would he?'

'He came back to find his skateboard,' said Trude, turning to me with wide eyes. 'But it's too late cos we've got it. It's all falling into place.'

'I guess.' I felt like crying.

'Think hard. Could it have been him at the statue?'

I shrugged. All I could dredge up was the image of a dark blur and a backpack. 'I suppose it *could* have been him, but I just don't know.'

Trude took my arm, propelling me to my feet. 'We'll work out a way of finding out for sure. If it is him, he won't get away with it.'

The thing was, I didn't want it to be him.

Chapter Eight

My key was already in the lock when the front door flew open.

'Dad!' I flung myself into his strong arms for a long overdue bear hug.

'Hello, poppet. How's my favourite girl?'

'Great,' I said, breathing in the Dad-smell from his jacket. Because suddenly everything *was* great. 'When did you get here?'

'Half an hour ago.' Dad was grinning like crazy, looking the same as he always did. His clothes were crumpled and his hair was a messy brown mop, though a few grey wisps were poking through.

'You've got pink cheeks,' he said with a chuckle. 'Must be the sea air. I said it would do you good being here.'

I wanted to chuckle with him, but for a second I couldn't speak. Dad seemed to understand. He squashed me against his chest and I felt the solid *thumpity-thump* of his heartbeat through his shirt.

'Is everything okay?' he said, finally pulling away and studying my face.

'I wish everyone would stop asking that.'

'We're just worried, Mallow. There's nothing we want more than for you to be safe and happy. I wish I were here more but you've always got Mum to talk to if you get anxious—'

Just then Mum bustled into the hall. Her eyes were bright and shiny with excitement. 'At last, you're here! Guess who I met on the way back from the beach?'

'Superman?' I said, catching Dad's eye.

He winked at me. 'Incredible Hulk?'

'No,' said Mum, tutting.

'I know, Spiderman!' I cackled.

'Stop it. You're both being silly,' said Mum, frowning. 'I met Laura Turner, one of the receptionists at the hospital. We recognised each other straightaway. She was with her daughter who goes to Framton Academy too . . . Faye?' Mum paused, waiting for me to nod. 'Anyway, Faye said she'd suggested a sleepover and asked if you were free tonight.'

My heart hopped into my throat. With everything else, I'd forgotten what Faye had suggested. 'What did you say?'

'That you weren't doing anything tonight, but I'd get you to call. I know you don't like the idea—'

'Why didn't you say I was busy?' I said. A 'sleepover' at Faye's house conjured up nightmare images of her German shepherd, Duke (more wolf than dog by the look of the photo on her Chat-Scape profile), waking me up as he mauled my wig. I could just see the looks of sheer horror on Faye's and Em's faces. 'Anyway, it's Dad's first night home.'

'Your decision, love,' said Mum. 'But I think it's a good idea.'

'Dad—'

'Sounds like fun,' said Dad slowly. 'Cal's going to Abraham's, and Mum and I've got a table booked at the Fresh Plaice on the prom. 'Bout time we had a meal out together. So, we'd all be sorted.'

'But I wanted to—'

'Plenty of time to catch up,' he said. 'I'm not going anywhere for a while.'

'And you might enjoy yourself,' said Mum. 'What do

you say? Give it a shot?'

'What about my wig?'

'You slept in your wig when you were sick that time, remember? And when we went camping. It didn't fall off.'

'But-say-it-does-this-time-what-will-I-do?' My words tumbled out in panic.

Mum took hold of my shoulders and fixed her eyes on mine. 'Mallow, nothing bad will happen. We can put extra tape on to make sure. And we'll put the Replenish on now so you don't have to take the tube. This is a big deal, love, I realise that. But you can always phone if things are getting too much for you. Dad or I will come and fetch you.'

'Mum, Faye doesn't even like me.'

'Then why would she invite you? She seemed keen. This could be her way of getting to know you better. Why not give her a chance?' Mum picked up my mobile and held it out to me. 'What happened before . . . I know it plays on your mind, but most people aren't like that. But I'm not going to force you, Mallow. Not if you don't want to. It's your choice.'

If I rang Faye, what would I say? 'Sorry, I don't want to come after all?' I'd seem all stuck up and I'd never live it down. Besides, Mum and Dad *did* deserve time alone

57

without me hanging around. BUT being discovered as a bald freak . . . My mind was made up. I seized the mobile from Mum. 'I can't go.'

'That's a shame,' she said. 'Oh well, there'll be other times. And Faye said something about a boy being round for the evening, so maybe she won't be too disappointed you won't be there.'

'What boy?' My finger was suspended over the call icon.

'I've no idea. Someone from your class – he's quite new too, she said.'

It had to be Dan. Trude had told me he'd joined not long before me and Em. My thoughts see-sawed.

If I went to Faye's, I'd see Dan.

I'd be spending time with him. THE WHOLE EVENING.

If he had it in for me, it would show, wouldn't it?

I stared at the phone in my hand. Perhaps I should give the sleepover a go. Mum and Dad would get time alone together. I'd get to speak to Dan face-to-face; I'd watch him like a hawk. It'd be my chance to suss out if he really *was* the one making my life a misery (*please, no*). By the end of the evening it'd be clear what I was up against.

Chapter Nine

Faye's mum wasn't how I imagined her. I thought she'd be all air kisses, pongy perfume and chunky gold jewellery, but this woman was wearing a floaty, layered skirt that reached almost to the ground. Like Faye, she had curly red hair, which she'd tied back, but strands had escaped over her forehead. Multicoloured bangles jangled on her wrist when she clasped my icy hand. 'You're struggling, my dear. But don't worry, all will be well. If you want your fortune read, you only need ask.'

'Laura, leave the girl alone.' A skinny man with a scruffy grey beard appeared in the kitchen doorway, a pair of binoculars dangling round his neck. 'I'm Sam.' He grinned at me and Mum. 'We haven't met before.' He held up a dead sparrow and Mum and I both jolted back, though

Laura kept hold of my hand. The bird's head flopped to the side and I couldn't help noticing the spot of blood on its tiny breast.

'That blasted cat's been at it again,' said Sam, drawing the bird back to his face to examine it. 'I swear I'll kill it the next time I catch the—'

'Don't be so melodramatic,' said Laura.

'I tell you, it'll be curtains. This carnage has to stop.' Sam stared at Mum.

'Well, it's certainly . . .' Mum faltered into silence.

Laura finally let my hand drop. 'Sam, I wish you wouldn't bring dead wildlife into the house. And you know full well that Faye would never forgive you if anything happened to Fabiola. Sorry, Mallow . . . Helen, what must you think of us?'

I had just enough time to give Mum a quick hug before Laura ushered me through to the sitting room. Faye and Em were slumped on the sofa with a huge bowl of popcorn balanced on a cushion between them. There was no sign of Dan. Their eyes were glued to a film playing on the huge TV screen. Faye's socked feet were propped on the coffee table. A pair of cherry-red Converse All Star trainers lay underneath, the same style as the tatty blue ones I had back in London, waiting to be packed up with the rest of my stuff. Faye's looked brand new.

'Hi,' said Faye, flicking a look in my direction. 'Grab a seat.'

It took me two seconds to realise that Faye's dog, Duke, was in the only other seat facing the TV. As I got near the armchair he raised his massive head and gave a low, throaty growl. His top lip curled to reveal a row of glistening teeth. We eyeballed each other and I resigned myself to sitting on the carpet as far away from him as possible. I didn't fancy having a chunk ripped from my leg.

'Get off there, stupid mutt,' ordered Faye.

Duke moved his bulk and flopped on the floor, right beneath the armchair. I manoeuvred around him and sat down, drawing my legs up to avoid treading on his tail.

'All right?' said Faye. She stuffed more popcorn in her mouth, then held the bowl out. I took a small handful.

'Yep.' Then, trying to sound casual, I said, 'I thought Dan was coming?'

'Oh, he can't make it after all,' said Faye, her mouth turned down at the corners. 'Said he had to do something with his dad.'

'Sounds like an excuse. Obviously there's a reason he didn't want to come,' said Em, her gaze drilling into mine. 'Wonder what it could be?'

Her comment didn't register to start with – my heart was too busy sinking. The whole point in me being there had been wiped out in an instant. Gone was my chance to get to know the *real* Dan. I wouldn't be able to check him out, to find out what his game was. And, as Em had hinted, was I the reason he'd pulled out? He couldn't face spending an evening with the girl he was sending creepy messages to? Or maybe he wasn't responsible for the messages at all (*great*), but still didn't want to see me (*not so great*). Either way, a long, hellish night yawned in front of me.

Faye and Em had obviously seen the film before and spent most of it giggling hysterically and swapping comments on what was going on. When I tried to join in with the conversation, I got blank stares followed by stupid tittering. By the time the credits rolled it felt as if it was well past midnight, but when I looked at the time it wasn't even 10 p.m.

Faye dumped the empty popcorn bowl on the coffee table and stretched. 'Come on, let's go to my room. Mum will nag if we play music down here.'

As we went into the hallway, I looked at my jacket slung over the bannister, wishing I could grab it and bolt. I had just put a hand on it when the kitchen door flew open and Laura appeared, a waft of incense billowing out behind her. Soft moaning came from the depths of the candlelit kitchen. For a moment, I wondered if Laura was in the middle of performing a weird ritual on the cat. Then I realised it was whale music, like they played in the New Age shops in Fossilworth.

'Not leaving, are you, Mallow?'

'Just checking my phone,' I mumbled and turned to trudge up the stairs.

Unlike the rest of the house, Faye's room was super tidy: the floor clear of clothes and the books lined up on shelves, ordered according to height. Under the shelves was a polished wooden desk with a swivel chair. Faye obviously had a thing for green because the stationery on the desk was entirely that colour. A wicker swing chair with plump cushions hung from a brass hook in the ceiling.

When Faye opened her wardrobe, everything was hanging in colour-coordinated rows. She laughed at my stunned expression. 'I like it this way,' she said, moving towards the bed and smoothing out a wrinkle from the lime-green duvet. Em dived backwards onto it, her limp, brown hair mushrooming around her.

'Is this where I'm sleeping?' Em asked, stretching like a cat and stroking a hand over the duvet cover.

'Nope,' said Faye, unfolding a foam chair and turning it into a mattress. One of the shelves in the wardrobe was stacked with bedding. She grabbed some and tossed them on top of Em. 'I'll find the blow-up bed for you, Mallow. Back in a sec.'

'I don't mind being in the spare room,' I said quickly. 'I snore – I wouldn't want to keep you awake.'

'What's the point of a sleepover if you're not in the same room as us?' said Em.

'Just thought I'd mention it.' I forced a smile.

'Don't worry,' said Faye, as she headed for the door. 'Nothing keeps me awake.'

The door clicked shut, and I was alone with Em. The temperature seemed to drop ten degrees. There was an awkward silence.

'Guess you're disappointed Dan didn't come?' said Em, all of a sudden.

'Not really,' I lied.

Em sniffed, then said, 'I used to live in London.' She inspected the nails of her left hand. 'Not far from where you lived.'

'Oh.' An icy block wedged itself in my tummy. 'How do you know that?'

'Trude told me. Chiswick, right?' Em propped herself

up on her elbows and looked at me with her cool grey eyes.

'Right.' I didn't like Em having one bit of information, however small, about my old life.

Another silence.

'Where did the name Mallow come from?' asked Em.

'A plant.'

'Your mum and dad named you after a plant?'

'Well, the flower. Like Rose or Violet.'

'But Mallow is . . . different.'

I knew what she meant by different: weird.

'I like it,' I said. That wasn't strictly true – I LOVED the name Mum and Dad had given me. It was quirky and unique and made me feel special.

Faye was taking ages. I pulled out the stool in front of her dressing table and saw a photo of a black cat with a white striped nose lodged between the mirror and its frame. Fabiola, I guessed. Faye had an incredible collection of brightly coloured nail varnishes, pots of eyeshadow and lip balm, all lined up three deep in front of the mirror.

'Here.' Faye's reflection appeared behind me. She had one of the little pots in her hand. 'Let me give you a quick makeover.'

'I don't wear much make-up,' I said, my heart racing.

'I've noticed,' said Faye. 'It won't take a minute.'

Before I had time to protest, Faye twisted me round so my back was to the mirror, ordered me to shut my eyes and started rubbing something on the lids. Her face was so near mine that her warm breath tickled my cheeks and nose. *What if she spots the wig?* I scrunched my hands into tight balls, my nails digging into the flesh of my palms.

'Relax.' Faye laughed. 'You're kind of uptight.'

'Yeah,' said Em. 'Didn't you do this with your friends in London?'

I couldn't answer. My heart was thumping so hard I thought it would pop out of my mouth.

'There.' Faye finally turned me back round to face the mirror. 'Much better. Though you looked fine before,' she added after a beat.

I turned my head to one side and then the other and admired my profile. She hadn't done a bad job. She'd highlighted my lips and eyes. A dab of blusher on each cheek bone gave my pale face some colour. The make-up looked good; I looked good.

Em got up and came to stand next to Faye, staring hard at me. 'Cool. Do you ever wear your hair up?'

'No . . .' I didn't like where this conversation was going.

'You should try it.' Em's gaze shifted in Faye's direction and back again to me, her smirk reflected in the mirror. 'I'm sure *Dan* would love it.'

Why did she mention Dan again? 'I'm not bothered, really.' I wiped my sweaty palms on my jeans.

'Let me have a go.' Em went to grab a bunch of my hair.

'No!' I sprung up from the stool and it tipped backwards, crashing into Em's shins.

'Ouch!' she yelped. 'Careful, you idiot. What's your problem?'

'Come on, Em,' said Faye. 'It was an accident.'

'Sorry, I'm . . .' I stopped and took a shaky breath. 'I . . . need the bathroom . . .' Faye gestured to a door next to the wardrobe, and I dashed into the en suite and rammed the bolt across. I leant over the toilet, my insides churning like a washing machine. At last I straightened up and splashed water on my face. So much for the make-up, but the coolness helped me recover. I gazed at myself in the mirror. My face was ashen except for the streams of black mascara running down my cheeks. I grabbed a wad of Faye's cotton wool and tried to mop up the mess. The wig looked the same as always – thick and glossy. For one wild moment I was tempted to rip the hateful thing off my scalp and flush it down the toilet.

'Get a grip,' I told my reflection. After thirty seconds of deep, slow breathing, my heart rate had returned to normal. I gripped the edge of the basin and stared at the scared girl in the wig looking back at me. I didn't want to be her, but the real me had vanished.

I heard muffled whispering, followed by a rap on the door.

'Are you all right in there?' Faye's voice, louder now, came from right outside. She sounded worried. It took me a few seconds to decide what to do. Then I threw the bolt back and shuffled into the bedroom, past an astonished Faye, clutching my stomach and groaning. Em and Faye both stared at me.

'What's the matter?' said Em.

'Sorry 'bout that,' I croaked. 'Not well. I'd better go home.'

Em and Faye exchanged glances. 'Two minutes ago you were fine,' said Em, crossing her arms.

'Well, I'm not now.' Without waiting for a reply, I picked up my bag and legged it downstairs, grabbing my jacket from the bannister.

'Are you okay?' I spun round and came face-to-face

with Laura. She stood in the kitchen doorway with a mug in her hand. The whale music had stopped but the smell of incense drifted around her like an invisible mist. Duke was standing by her side. He gave a low growl.

I shook my head. 'I'm going home. I don't feel well.'

'Oh dear, perhaps you've picked up the bug that's going around?'

'Maybe,' I muttered, not able to meet her eye.

'Let me drive you,' she said, stepping into the hall. 'My shoes must be somewhere. Or Sam will. Sam!'

'No, it's fine. Dad'll collect me. I'll wait outside though. I'm still feeling dizzy.'

'If you're sure,' said Laura. 'You do look pale. Wait a minute – I'll come out with you.'

'No, don't,' I said quickly. 'I mean, I'm fine – I just need some air.'

'Well, all right,' said Laura, looking doubtful. 'If you change your mind, come back in. It's freezing out there.'

I nodded and then I was outside, taking great gulps of cold, fresh air. I called Dad on his mobile and perched, miserable and chilled, on the low brick wall bordering the front garden. While waiting for Dad to arrive, I messaged Trude with the whole sorry sleepover story. She replied with a sad face and said she'd talk to me in the morning,

as her cousins were staying over. *Great*. I heaved a sigh –
just when I needed to talk to her. The evening had been
disastrous. I shouldn't have come. Dan hadn't been there,
and Faye and Em didn't believe I was ill. I glanced up
towards Faye's bedroom window and caught a glimpse of two
faces peering down at me. Then the curtain closed.

Chapter Ten

It seemed as if I'd had only MINUTES of sleep when Mum woke me the morning after the non-sleepover. She pulled open the curtains to let in the winter sun, put a cup of tea beside me and sat on my bed stroking the back of my hand.

Dad had tried talking to me last night in the car, but I'd spent most of the short journey blubbing. By the time we'd got home I'd calmed down a bit. Mum had made me hot chocolate, and they'd both sat with me while I told them what had gone so wrong at Faye's.

'Horrid wig . . . *sob* . . . make-up . . . *sniff* . . . freak . . . *bawl*.' Mum had shushed and hugged me tight like she used to do when I was little. Eventually I'd managed to stop snivelling and she had helped me into my pyjamas and into bed.

Now she watched as I drank the tea.

'I thought you and I could go out to lunch. Perhaps to the French bistro in Fossilworth. How does that sound?'

'Muh,' I said, my attempt at mixing a yes with a maybe. I slurped my tea.

'And why don't we set about decorating your room? It's a bit of a dump, isn't it? We could get some colour charts today.' She swiped her fringe out of her eyes. 'What do you fancy? Mint green? Lilac? The whole house needs a revamp, to be honest, but we'll start in here. What do you say?'

I squinted a yes at her from between my puffy eyelids. Then Mum was saying that Faye and Em would soon forget last night (*as if*), and that Dad would make me pancakes for breakfast to cheer me up.

But NOTHING would cheer me up.

Mum kissed my cheek, then made to leave.

'Mum.' I stretched my arms out. I saw her face relax and she leant into me for a hug. We stayed like that for a minute, Mum rubbing small circles on my back. I squeezed my eyes shut, willing the tears away. Eventually we let each other go.

'Right, I'll take this washing down,' said Mum, her voice shaky. 'You get up and have some breakfast.'

I watched Mum collect my dirty clothes and dash out of the room. Then I lay staring at the web of spidery cracks that criss-crossed the ceiling. I tried to concentrate on nice things, like what a great friend Trude was and how good it was having Dad home, but every few seconds an ugly image from the night before slid to the front of my mind. I'd overreacted, I knew I had. Why did I have to panic every time anyone went near my head? Why had I run away like that? Facing Faye and Em at school on Monday was going to be a nightmare.

In the end, thoroughly sick of the thoughts looping round my head, I decided to get up. Cocooned in the duvet, I hopped out of bed, squealing as my feet hit the icy floorboards. I shuffled over to the radiator. Stone cold. I yanked the radiator knob one way then the other, but it wouldn't budge. I needed heat before I dared to get dressed in the Arctic cold. There was only one thing to do. Gran kept a fan heater in her bedroom for 'chilly nights'.

It felt wrong intruding in Gran's private space. The room smelt of stuffiness and the lavender drawer liners she liked to use. Framed prints of me and Cal stood on the dusty dressing table. I must have been about eight when the one of me was taken. I was wearing a swimming costume and beaming like an idiot into the camera. There was a frame containing a card I'd made when Gran was sick last year. It was a sketch of a bunch of flowers, done at my old school. It wasn't very good and I hadn't even known she'd kept it. Gran didn't have much other personal stuff in her room. It looked a bit gloomy. If it'd been my bedroom I'd have brightened it up with some posters or flowers or something, although Gran had been in hospital so long any flowers would have been dead by now.

The fan heater stood in front of the radiator, by the window. As I crouched to unplug it, I spotted a piece of glossy card poking out from behind the radiator pipes. I found one of Gran's knitting needles and jabbed it through the gap to dislodge the card.

It was a photo with yellowing edges, the colours orange and faded with time. I recognised Gran's drawing room – the fireplace and floor-to-ceiling windows – but by the look of the furniture, it'd been taken years ago. The woman in the picture looked like Mum – the same oval-shaped face and slightly too large nose – but something in the way her head tilted to the side was different. On the back of the photo was some crabby, scrunched-up handwriting: 'Me and Helen at home. August, 1969.' The woman had to be a younger Gran. Dressed in a beige skirt and white blouse, with a pink scarf wrapped around her head like a turban, she looked as if she was about to go out somewhere. On the floor by her feet was a baby, reaching out a chubby hand. The photo must have lain behind the radiator for years. With the heater forgotten, I turned around and headed for the stairs, photo in hand to show Mum.

Chapter Eleven

Everyone was in the kitchen when I went downstairs. Cal was sitting at the table crunching cocoa pops while Mum tapped away at her laptop.

Dad was fiddling with an old radio. 'Gran's been complaining it doesn't work,' he explained. 'How're you feeling, poppet?'

'Better,' I said, bending down to rescue a screwdriver that had fallen on the floor. I placed it and the old photo on the worktop.

'Good stuff.' Dad grinned. 'Fancy taking Bilbo for a walk with me later?'

'Sure.' Time alone with Dad could be just what I needed. It would be my chance to mention the messages.

'What's this?' Dad picked up the photo. 'It looks old.'

'I found it.'

'Cool,' said Cal, coming over to Dad's side. 'Hey, Mum, are you the baby in the picture?'

'Goodness,' said Mum. 'Yes, it's me with Gran. Funny, I didn't think she'd kept any old photos of herself. She's always said they're "sentimental tosh" and that she never looked good in them. Show her when she comes home, Mallow. I'm sure she'd be interested.'

'Do you think Gramps took the picture?' I said.

'He must have done.' Mum smiled. 'Poor Gramps. I remember he'd spend ages persuading Gran to pose. He used to try to sneak up on her when she wasn't expecting it, just so he could take a shot. Didn't often work though.'

'What's that thing on her head?' asked Cal.

'It's called a hat,' I said, rolling my eyes.

'She liked wearing hats and scarves,' said Mum. 'I'd forgotten that.'

'There's the monkey puzzle tree in the garden,' said Cal.

When I looked again I could make out its trunk through the tall window.

'Looks just the same.' He peered closer at the picture. 'Apart from that grey splodge. I think it's a squirrel.'

'Get your mucky fingers off, Cal,' I said, pulling it

away from him. 'You'll ruin it.' I pocketed the photo, planning to stash it in my memory box later.

'Pancakes?' asked Dad. 'I'll quickly whip up the batter.'

'Don't bother for me. I'm too hungry to wait,' I said, my stomach growling on cue.

Dad laughed. 'You're not kidding. What have you got in there, a bear cub?'

I giggled as I opened the cereal cupboard and reached for the Weetaflakes. I stopped. 'Mum, what are those?' The top shelf was cluttered with tubs, small bottles and tubes. They weren't food items. And they definitely hadn't been there yesterday.

'Ah . . .' said Mum. 'I was waiting for the right moment.'

'For what?'

Mum hesitated for a second. 'Let's talk about it when you're feeling brighter.'

'I'm fine. I want to know now.' I pulled down a couple of the small bottles.

'Okay.' Mum slowly removed her glasses and placed them on the worktop. 'They're hair loss treatments.'

I stared at her.

Her cheeks were pink. 'I know I've gone overboard,

but I said I'd find something, didn't I?'

'Wow, they're . . .' I didn't know what to say, so I examined the bottles instead. When I held them up to the light I could see a mass of tiny circular pills. 'I don't want to be experimented on. I'm not a guinea pig.'

'Don't be ridiculous,' said Mum, as she tucked a wisp of hair behind one ear. 'They're perfectly safe.'

I glared at her.

'Seriously, Mallow. One of these might be the answer. And if they don't work, we'll give proper thought to the States.'

'What's this about the States?' Dad piped up. 'Nice of you to mention it to me.'

'It's just an idea, Dave,' said Mum. 'I haven't had the chance to talk to you about it . . . since you're never here.'

'Not got a lot of choice, have I?'

Great. They're fighting because of me.

'It's a cool idea!' said Cal. 'Can we go to Universal Studios?'

'That's not the point of it,' snapped Mum, returning to her laptop. 'Anyway, there'd be loads to sort out before we decided anything. Not least your gran.' She patted the chair next to her. I sat with a thump. 'I was going to tell you about this at a better time, but since you've asked . . .

I've made a chart.' Mum pointed at a complicated-looking spreadsheet on the screen. 'To keep a log of which treatment you're using, how long you've been on it, and the dosage. We'll plot your progress. See, I've entered the one you started the other day.'

I studied the list. Mum had covered the whole range – from freaky herbal drinks to homoeopathic hair tonics to vitamin tablets.

'Helen,' said Dad, 'Mallow may not want to try quack remedies . . .'

'These are not quack remedies,' said Mum. 'They've all been tested and got positive reviews online.'

'Okay, okay,' said Dad, throwing his hands up in mock-defence. 'At the end of the day, it's up to Mallow.'

'You want to keep trying, don't you, love?'

When I finally managed to speak, my words sounded weird, as if coming from a far-off planet. 'Where did you get this stuff?'

'Most of them are from Faye's mum – she gave me a whole bagful last night. She's into healing. Don't worry,' she said, clocking my expression. 'She thinks Dad's the one who needs it!'

I wished Mum hadn't talked to Laura. Dad still had a full head of hair – Laura would puzzle out the truth in five minutes flat. I'd just have to hope she didn't bump into him in the next twenty years.

Dad plugged the radio in. 'There, that's sorted. If no one wants pancakes, I'll do some gardening now. Let me know when you're ready for that walk, Mallow.' He ducked through the back door.

'You don't have to do this,' said Mum as she looked up from the computer. 'But it's like anything in life – if you don't try, you'll never know. You do want a treatment that works, don't you?'

'Yeah, but it's pointless cos they *never* work.'

'We can crack this, Mallow. Let's give it a go.'

Mum smiled at me, so I shrugged. A cure for the alopecia was what I wanted, wasn't it? But a niggling little voice kept bleating in my ear, *Doesn't Mum love me the way I am?*

In my room later, I placed Gran's photo in my memory box. Inside were mementos I'd collected over the years: a lock of my real hair in a little see-through bag, birthday cards, holiday souvenirs, a lucky penny and the hair clip Gran had given me for my twelfth birthday, before I'd developed alopecia. Gran had never really bothered with my and Cal's birthdays before. Five pounds stuffed in an envelope had been as good as it had got. I'd been surprised by the clip wrapped in pink tissue paper and tied with a ribbon. It was a tiny Welsh dragon of little red crystals set into a silver casing, with a minute green gemstone for an eye.

'No use to me now. I don't go anywhere fancy enough to wear it,' Gran had said when she'd handed it to me. 'It was given to me by *my* grandmother when I turned twelve. You might as well have it.'

'Don't worry,' she'd said to Cal. 'There's something for you when you reach the right age too.'

The present reminded me that poor Gran was stuck in the hospital, all alone. I replaced the dragon clip in the box. One day, when my hair grew back, I'd wear it again.

Chapter Twelve

Monday lunchtime, and the canteen buzzed with people queueing for food. As I joined the back of the line, I spotted Dan with Fraser and Archie. A group of Year Sevens were squeezed between us, making it easier to lurk without being noticed. I pretended to examine the seeded buns in the chiller cabinet as I strained to eavesdrop over the chatter.

'Mate, you're missing out. Crusade is the best game out there,' Archie was saying.

'Computer's wrecked,' said Dan. 'Since the move. Nothing works properly.'

'You seriously need to get your stuff sorted. Then you can play with me and Fraser.'

'Want me to come over and check it out?' said Fraser.

'I'm good at mending tech.'

'Nah. Think it's had it.' Dan sounded rattled. I squinted sideways. His face looked even paler than normal. 'I'm saving up for a new one.'

'Your loss,' said Fraser, shrugging one shoulder. 'There's not much I can't fix.'

A squeal distracted me from the conversation. I turned and realised I'd been squishing one of the Year Sevens against the chiller cabinet in my effort to get close enough to hear the boys.

'Sorry,' I murmured. Now Dan's chocolate eyes were on me. I gave a nervous grin.

'You've dropped your sandwich.' Dan pushed through the Year Sevens and picked it up.

I felt my face go red as I took it from him.

'You drop things a lot,' Dan remarked, just as Archie clapped him on the shoulder. Dan moved back into his place in the queue.

After paying, I made my way outside. Trude was sitting at one of the picnic tables, flicking through a magazine. I gave her the squashed sandwich. There could be loads of reasons why Dan didn't want Fraser and Archie at his house. But at that precise moment I couldn't think of one.

Trude wrinkled her nose. 'Did you step on this?'

'Sorry. Can't have made it taste worse than it normally does.'

Trude shrugged and took a bite. 'Do you want to come to mine after school?' she said with her mouth full. 'We can talk business.'

'What?' My mind was still on Dan.

'The business,' said Trude. 'You said you'd help.'

'Oh, yeah. Okay.'

'Cool. I've got the dentist at five, but we'll still have over an hour.' She took another bite and gazed at me. 'Have you spoken to your dad about the messages?'

'Not yet.'

'You have to, hun. What's happening is wrong.'

'I know, I know. But Dad's being useless. It's so annoying.' The truth was, I'd been waiting to get him on his own, but Cal and Mum and DIY jobs kept getting in the way. Even the walk with Bilbo that Dad had suggested didn't happen because Mum wanted him to fix the dishwasher. 'He's always busy—'

'Trude, Trude!' Faye and Em were waving in our direction. It was the first time I'd seen them since the non-sleepover. I tried a welcoming smile but Faye ignored me and made a beeline for Trude, squishing up next to her on the bench.

Em crossed her arms and said, 'Feeling better?'

I fiddled with my fringe to check it was in place. 'Yeah, thanks.'

'Sudden, wasn't it?'

'What?'

'Your illness. Came on suddenly.'

I shrugged. 'Guess so.'

For a moment it looked as if she was going to add something, but then she glanced away.

'Ta-dah!' Faye produced a shimmering, blue A4 piece of paper from behind her back. 'I did these in art club. Miss Reach asked me to staple them on the noticeboards to replace the horrid school ones. But I had to show you first, Trude. Can you believe it's not even two weeks away?'

I tried to read the paper that Faye fluttered in front of Trude. It was dotted with little silver stars and snowflakes. I caught sight of the words 'Year Nine Charity Christmas Ball' in spidery writing on the shiny background.

Faye laid the poster on the picnic table and I read the rest.

'Friday, 8th December at 8 p.m. Tickets £5. Proceeds to the Wishing Well Children's Fund.'

Trude had been talking about the ball for weeks. Beth's mum was in the PTA and it had been her idea to hold a charity ball every year instead of the usual disco. *All* of Year Nine went. Even if you were dead you'd still be expected to turn up in your coffin. It was *the* event of the year and missing it meant you'd be cast into the desert of friendlessness forever.

A small part of me *had* been looking forward to it. That was, until the messages had started.

'Someone gets chosen to do a speech, too,' said Trude. 'That's a bit lame, but they get a prize for doing it. Last year it was fifty pounds.'

'Can't wait,' said Faye, pushing her glasses higher up her pointy nose. 'I'm going to get my nails done at that new place. Want to come too, Trude?'

'Great!' said Trude. She clutched Faye's arms and pumped them up and down.

'Hey, am I invited?' said Em.

'Course,' said Faye, her freckly cheeks turning scarlet. 'You know you are.'

'And you too, Mallow,' said Trude. 'We'll have to sort our outfits too. Finding something to wear will take ages.'

'My mum said she'd hire a posh limo for us,' said Em.

'Cool,' said Trude, who was now jigging up and down with glee.

'Yeah, they'll be room for you, Trude, with me, Faye,

Archie, Fraser and Dan, if he wants.'

'And Mallow,' said Trude, clapping her hands.

Faye carefully rolled up the poster.

Em gave a little giggle. 'Thing is, the car won't take more than six.'

'Come on, Em,' said Trude, stopping mid-jig. Her ears had gone a fiery red. 'Fraser and Archie can go by themselves. They won't mind. There's got to be room for Mallow.'

'Guess we could squeeze you in somewhere, couldn't we?' said Faye. She nudged Em with her elbow. 'What do you think?'

Em inflated her cheeks and puffed out. 'I'll ask, but I really don't know.'

'It's okay,' I said, swallowing the marble-sized lump in my throat. 'I can make my own way there.'

Trude nibbled her lip. It was obvious she wanted to go with the others but was having a guilt trip about me.

I produced my brightest smile. 'It's not a problem. Really. Mum will give me a lift.'

'Are you sure?' said Em, sounding over the moon. 'I mean, you'll be better off with your mum, seeing as it would be so squashed.' And then, grudgingly. 'But I'll ask if you want.'

Make me feel welcome, why don't you? 'It's fine.'

'That's sorted,' said Faye. She glanced between me and Em, looking relieved. 'Can't wait!' The two of them hurried off.

Trude gazed at me. 'I won't go in the limo either, hun. I'll go with you.'

'Doesn't matter,' I said with a thick voice. Though inside it did matter. Memories of Sara *(how could I have ever called her my best friend?)* and 'that lot'. The way they'd made me feel so lonely and sad. Faye and Em hadn't been exactly friendly since I arrived, and now they'd become positively glacial. Though after my behaviour at Faye's house the other night it wasn't a surprise. Em didn't believe I'd been sick and now they thought I was a complete weirdo.

'Don't think I'll be going to the ball anyway,' I added. 'Not if the message creep is still at large.'

Trude wrapped an arm around me. 'But you have to come – I won't take no for an answer. Who cares about that stupid creep? I'll take care of you. You'll look gorgeous.'

My phone pinged.

I know what you did at your old school.

The words blurred as I stared at them. Suddenly I was

back there in the school pool. I could taste the bitter water, hear the screaming, remember fingers clawing at my face, thrashing legs kicking against mine . . .

'What's up?' said Trude. She peered over my shoulder at the screen. 'Oh hun, how could anyone from here have found out about *that*?'

'I don't know.' I held my head in my hands, trying to steady my breathing. My mind was rioting. 'Did you tell anyone?'

'Course not.' Trude frowned. 'You know I wouldn't do that, right?'

'Yeah, sorry.' I blushed.

Another bleep.

The ball's gonna be such fun!

'We'll sort this.' Trude stuffed her sandwich wrapper between the slats of the picnic table, and snatched the phone from me.

'What are you doing?' I squeaked and grabbed it back.

'I was going to tell the creep to get lost,' she said.

'Wait, I'll do it.' I tapped in a message:

Back off. We're on to you.

I took a deep breath and pressed 'Send'.

'Right, now there must be a way of blocking the number, even on this ancient thing,' said Trude. 'I'll ask

Fraser how to do it.'

'No, don't. He'll want to know why. Anyway, if I block the number I'll never find out who's sending the messages.'

'If I were you—'

'I know,' I said.

I fished Trude's wrapper out from the slats in the table and flung it in a nearby bin. Sending a message had been a brave move; what if it backfired and pushed the creep to post on Chat-Scape?

But I had to *do* something.

Chapter Thirteen

I reached for my school bag as the bell went for the end of lunch. 'I'm going to check Dan out after school, see where he goes. The skateboard's in my locker. I'll take it with me and confront him. Want to come?'

'I thought we were going to mine to talk about the business.'

'Can we do it another time?'

Trude's face fell. 'Oh, okay.'

'I mean, I really want to help, but I need to sort this out.'

Trude hesitated. 'It's fine. You go ahead. I've got the dentist at five anyway, so it's probably best I don't come with you.' She picked up her bag and turned away. 'I'll see you tomorrow. You can tell me about it then.'

'Trude—'

She waved a hand as she walked off. I shrugged.

*

At the end of school I took up a position in the bushes outside the gates. A whole freezing twenty minutes later, when I'd almost given up, Dan appeared with Fraser and Archie. They said goodbye and Fraser and Archie went one way while Dan stomped right past my hiding place. Stomped, I noted shakily, because he didn't have his skateboard. That was right next to me, in the bushes.

I waited until Dan was well down East End Road before I set off after him. He strode towards the seafront, but instead of turning onto the prom as I expected, he went along the narrow pavement, past the crazy golf course and under the railway bridge. The road curved away from the coast here, and scrubby fields hid the view of the sea. I hadn't walked this way before, though it was the route we took in the car to see Gran in hospital in Fossilworth.

I'd been following Dan for fifteen minutes and the skateboard was getting awkward to carry. It kept banging against my hip and every few paces I had to shift it from one arm to the other. The chilly air made my legs ache, and the light was fading. All the while, I worried that Dan would spin round and spot me, but he kept plodding on with his collar turned up and his hands shoved deep in his pockets.

At last he made a left turn onto a muddy track that was bordered by a thick, scratchy hedge. After another five minutes of traipsing he reached a metal gate, went through and shut it with a clank.

Slipping and sliding, I reached the gate. I expected to see a house or garden the other side, but instead it led into a boggy field of long grass, with a thick line of trees at the far end. Perhaps Dan lived behind the trees, but how had he disappeared so quickly? I dithered at the gate. Water had seeped through the thin soles of my shoes and my feet squelched with even the slightest movement. I'd told Mum I was going to the library after school. She'd expect me back soon. Ever since London, she got stressy if I didn't turn up on time.

I was on the verge of giving up when a movement to my left caught my attention. There was a small caravan tucked in the corner of the field. It was almost hidden by overgrown brambles and bushes, which would explain why I hadn't spotted it sooner. Dan was standing in the entrance, staring straight at me.

'What are you doing here?' he called. Unsurprisingly, he didn't look happy to see me.

'Uh.' For a moment my brain struggled to come up with one reason I'd be standing in the same swampy field as him without sounding like a stalker. At last, I remembered the skateboard propped under my arm. 'I came to return this. Yours, isn't it?'

'Where did you find it?' Dan asked. I followed his gaze down to the muddy puddle around my ankles. 'You'd better come in.'

I wavered. If Dan was the message sender, I was on the verge of walking into his lair, and that spelt DANGER.

But a huge part of me still didn't believe Dan was the one. This might be my best chance of proving it.

And I *was* half frozen from the cold.

'Coming or what?'

I squelched through the mud and up the caravan steps. I saw a pair of dirty boots lying on a wodge of newspaper in the entrance, so I slipped my pumps off and left them on the paper, along with the skateboard. The soles of my tights were sopping wet but there was no way I was going to take those off. I continued into the van, leaving a trail of soggy footprints on the vinyl floor.

Without saying a word, Dan jerked his head towards the U-shaped bench at the end, and then turned to fill a kettle. I slid onto the bench, my cheeks burning, and wondered whether I'd made a big mistake.

'You'd make a rubbish private eye,' said Dan, his gaze at last meeting mine.

'You knew I was following you?' And I'd thought I'd been so careful.

He nodded. 'Spotted you a mile off.'

'Do you live here on your own?'

He snorted. 'Course not. Dad's here too.' Then, 'My mum left us,' he continued, predicting my next question. 'She couldn't live with Dad's ways.'

'Sorry.'

He shrugged.

'But how come . . . Why are you . . . ?'

'We're not travellers, if that's what you think. It's temporary. We got chucked out of our last place and this van belongs to Dad's mate. The field is part of his farm. He's letting us stay here for nothing until Dad gets a second job.' He pointed to a small, framed watercolour propped against the window behind the table. 'Dad's an artist. That's one of his.' The painting showed a hillside dotted with fluffy, cotton-ball sheep and what looked like a ruined stone mill in the background.

'It's beautiful. Where is that?'

'Up on the moors, beyond Fossilworth,' said Dan. 'We

go there at weekends so he can sketch.'

'Does he sell many?' I picked the frame up to admire the painting.

'Can do, depends. The souvenir shops in town sell them and he's got a studio above the art shop, so they take a few there too. Now the tourist season is over, sales haven't been good so we had to move in here. There, you can go back and tell your mates all about me now.' He stuck out his lower jaw.

'I didn't . . . I wasn't following to . . .' Words fluttered out of my mouth. My brain felt as soggy as my feet.

'Whatever.' Dan turned his back. He opened a biscuit tin, then set it on the table in front of me.

'This place is cool!' I said, trying to ease the tension. 'No one else I know lives in a caravan.' The van was small – the whole thing was only about as long as my bedroom at Gran's, but half the width – and shabby. Up the other end, through an opening in the partition wall, I spotted an unmade double bed and a door to what I guessed was the toilet. But despite it being scruffy, everything had its place. When Dan opened one of the wall cupboards, I saw plates, bowls and cups stacked on the shelf. A piece of wood was nailed along the edge, presumably to stop them falling out when the caravan was on the move. Not that it looked as if the van had moved anytime in the last thirty years. Dan slid open another door and brought out teabags.

'Try living here twenty-four seven,' he said, putting two mugs on the worktop and opening a small fridge underneath.

'Is this place –' I gestured around the caravan – 'the reason you keep quiet about where you live?'

Dan gave a one-shoulder shrug. 'It's kind of embarrassing having to admit your home is a field. Some of the teachers know, but the last thing I need is Archie, Fraser and that lot ripping into me. I'd rather you didn't tell them either.'

'Course not, but I don't think they'd care where you live . . .' I stopped. My scalp was tingling, a reminder of my own hot little secret. Luckily, Dan hadn't noticed my sudden silence. He was busy sloshing milk in the mugs of tea. He brought them over to the table.

'There're plenty of worse things than living in a caravan,' I said at last.

Dan gave me a weird look. 'Yeah.'

I didn't say anything else, but he didn't seem to expect more. Instead, he sat on the bench seat opposite me. 'So how come you moved to Framton? From London, wasn't it?'

Taking a deep breath, I explained Gran's illness, Mum's sudden announcement and our move into Gran's house, while Dan hooked the teabags out with a spoon and plonked a mug in front of me.

'Must have been tough, leaving your friends behind,' he said, then thrust a whole biscuit into his mouth.

I grasped the steaming mug in both hands and stared into its murky depths as if I could read a hidden message in the tea. 'Not really,' I mumbled. Then I saw the open curiosity on his face. 'I mean, yes, but I was excited to be coming somewhere different. And I already knew Trude, from visiting Gran.'

Another silence while he finished munching, then: 'So if it wasn't to find out where I live, why follow me? It wasn't to give me my board back, cos you could have done that at school.'

'Er . . .'

'Wait a sec.' He got up. 'There're chocolate biscuits somewhere.'

Get a grip, I told myself, watching him rummaging in the cupboard again. *You've got to do this.* Now that I was sitting in his cosy caravan, doing normal-ish stuff like drinking tea and eating his biscuits, my suspicions seemed even crazier. Plus, I now knew why he acted so weirdly at school.

Dan returned to the table with a pack of chocolate digestives. 'So, spill. Why come out here with my old board? I'm grateful and all that – couldn't work out what I'd done with it – but actually I already bought a better one with money from my mum.' He gazed at me, waiting for an answer.

My mouth was dry. 'Some creep's been messaging me,' I blurted, before I could stop myself. 'Trude and I trailed them to the crazy golf course, and when they ran away, they left the skateboard.'

His eyebrows shot up, disappearing under his shaggy fringe. 'So, you put two and two together and assumed it was me? Logical, I guess, but I haven't been near the crazy golf. No good for skateboarding. I skate on the prom. And I've lost my mobile, so I can't send messages to anyone.'

I examined his face as he slurped the tea. He didn't look as if he was lying.

'Do you remember where you last had your board?'

Dan pressed his lips together as he considered the question. 'I'm pretty sure I met Fraser and Archie on Saturday. We went to the caff. I might have left it there.'

'The Black Cat?'

'Yeah,' he said. 'Drives my dad nuts, me losing stuff.'

'And it's driving me nuts not knowing who is . . .' I stopped.

Dan's head cocked to one side like a dog's. 'Gonna tell me more? Maybe I can help.'

'Sorry, I can't,' I said, fiddling with my mug. 'It's . . . personal stuff.'

He shrugged. 'Suit yourself. Let me know if you change your mind.'

Dan took another biscuit and dipped it in his tea. So much for Trude's theory. Someone was playing spiteful games but it didn't fit with the boy with messy hair sitting in front of me now, looking slightly baffled. If I ruled Dan out, I was no closer to finding the real culprit.

BUT IT WASN'T DAN. He'd convinced me of that. And it made my heart leap.

I took a deep breath and changed the subject. 'So, are you going to the ball?'

'Got to. Or Archie and Fraser will never let it drop,' he said. 'Though how I'll get there without getting covered in mud, I've no idea.'

'Change at mine, if you want,' I burst out, feeling heat swish across my scalp. My fingers flew up to smooth my hair. I wished the rickety floor would open up and swallow me. Why did I make that offer? I wasn't even sure I was going to the ball myself. 'I mean, you don't have to . . .'

'Thanks. I'll think about it,' he said slowly. 'Could be the answer.'

I took a gulp of tea and spluttered as it scalded my tongue.

'How's the drink?'

'Nice,' I mumbled between burnt lips.

'Dad says I make rubbish tea.' He grinned, and my edginess melted away.

Chapter Fourteen

'Can't believe Dan's not our man!' said Trude as we walked to the Black Cat café after school the next day.

'I know. Now I have no idea who it is.'

'Are you sure it isn't Dan, hun? He could just be a good liar.'

'I don't think he was lying.'

'What did you talk about then? Come on, there must be a bit of gossip.'

I kept my eyes on the pavement. 'There wasn't time to talk much.'

'*Really?*' said Trude, arching her eyebrows.

'I didn't mean that!' I said, feeling my cheeks flash pink. 'We just chatted about his dad's work.'

'*Boring!*' said Trude. 'So, where's his place?'

'In the middle of nowhere. On a farm.' Not exactly a lie; Dan *did* live on a farm, just not in the way Trude would imagine. Dan had got me to promise not to tell anyone about the caravan, and that had to include Trude. It made me uneasy. I was keeping more secrets than a government spy.

'Did you find out why he's so off with everyone?' said Trude. 'It's like he's got something to hide.'

'Search me.' I was desperate to get off the subject of Dan. 'One good thing, I've had no more messages.'

'Perhaps whoever it is has given up,' suggested Trude. 'And in that case, you'll be able to come to the ball without any problems!'

'Hmm, not sure . . .' I thought of my offer to Dan.

'I'm definitely giving the limo a miss, so we can go together.' Trude's voice sounded a bit weird.

'You fallen out with Faye?'

She gave a tiny shrug. 'I don't understand what's got into her – she's changed since she became friends with Em. It´s like she's one person with her and another with me. She used to be loads of fun.'

'I don't think Faye will ever like me,' I said. And at that precise moment, I wasn't bothered.

'She *is* nice when you get to know her,' said Trude. She

gave my arm a quick squeeze. 'And Em's . . . well . . . just being Em. Remember I told you she was at a boarding school in Switzerland?'

'Yeah?'

'Well, Faye said she got into trouble for stealing stuff from the other girls. And she kept running away because she hated it. She didn't fit in at all. Her parents just dumped her there and they hardly ever visited. Imagine that? She didn't even go home for holidays. I reckon she stole things to get their attention. They must have brought her back to England to sort her out. She went to some school in London, which didn't work out either, then they moved here. Makes you feel kind of sorry for her, doesn't it?' Trude linked her arm through mine.

I was going to disagree, but before I'd opened my mouth, Trude continued, 'Enough about Em. I want you and Faye, my two BEST friends, to be friends too. I'm sure you will be soon.'

I thought Faye wanting to be mates was as likely as Gran pogoing around the hospital ward. I didn't trust Faye. Maybe it was the way she looked at me – as if she was hatching a dark plan . . .

'Trude,' I said slowly. 'Has Faye ever said anything about me?'

'Like what?'

'She's off with me sometimes. And she and Em take things I've said the wrong way and act all offended.'

'What are you getting at?' Trude frowned.

'Nothing. I don't know.' I faltered. 'I just think it's suspicious, that's all.'

'Faye's been my friend for years. She'd never send horrid messages, if that's what you're thinking.' Trude tucked a loose strand of hair behind her ear. 'She and Em are just being prats about the limo. End of.'

'Yes, you're right, sorry,' I said, growing hot and bothered. 'Forget I mentioned it.'

'Anyway, you and I will go to the ball together and have a great time.'

'Yeah,' I said, trying to sound upbeat. 'We will.'

The waft of greasy bacon hit me as soon as we entered the café, making my insides flip. We wound our way between the grubby tables to the counter at the back. The floor was tacky under my shoes. Trude jerked her head towards a disgusting black blob and pulled a face. The usual grumpy woman was behind the counter thumbing through a magazine.

She glanced at us and pinched her lips into a paper-thin line. 'Yes?'

'Did a boy come in on Saturday?' I said, tripping over the words in my rush to get them out.

'You kids are always here,' said Grumpy Woman.

'He'd have had a skateboard,' I said. 'A scruffy one.'

'I wasn't here then.' The woman's voice oozed suspicion. 'Why do you want to know?'

'He thinks he left his board here by mistake. We said we'd pick it up for him.'

'Haven't seen it.'

'Perhaps whoever *was* here can tell us,' said Trude.

Grumpy Woman switched her stare to Trude. 'Lucy might remember.' And then she startled us both by yelling, 'Lu, come out here a sec; someone wants to ask you a question.'

'If it's Razor, the answer's still no,' came a voice from the back.

'Come out and tell him yourself,' shouted Grumpy Woman.

The door behind the counter swung open and a girl with dirty blonde hair appeared, rubbing her hands on an apron and chewing gum. After every couple of chomps her lips parted to reveal the sticky grey globule. 'Oh,' she said. 'Thought you were my ex.'

'Did a boy come in with a skateboard on Saturday?'

107

said Grumpy Woman. 'These girls want to know.'

Lu looked at us without interest, pulled the gum out and stuck it on a napkin on the counter. *Note to self: don't eat here, EVER.*

'Yeah,' she said at last. 'Made the counter dirty with it.'

It would have looked right at home, I thought.

'Dark-haired lad. Nice-looking,' Lu continued, grinning. 'If he'd been older . . . Anyway, he came in with a couple of boys, bought a can of coke. Then they left.'

'And he left the board behind?'

'Yeah.'

We waited for Lu to continue. She didn't.

'Have we got it still?' said Grumpy Woman.

Lu shook her head. She unwrapped another stick of gum. 'One of the girls took it.'

'What girls?' My heart pitter-pattered. I caught Grumpy Woman looking at me with an odd expression on her face. The tips of my ears were burning.

Lu shrugged. 'The girls who were here at the same time. They said they'd give it back to him.'

'What did they look like?'

'Didn't notice.'

Grumpy Woman snorted. 'As if. You're always snooping

on the customers.'

Lu looked daggers at Grumpy Woman and then said to me. 'One of them had hair like yours – blonde and really messy. The other was wearing a green bobble hat. That's all I can tell you.'

'Please, this is important.' My voice cracked. 'Which of them took the skateboard?'

'They left together, I think,' said Lu, but she didn't sound sure. She leant forwards, using her elbows as props. 'Do you go to Framton Academy? Is old Das Gupta still handing out detentions as if they were toffees?'

It was clear I was getting no more information, and I didn't want to get stuck talking about teachers at school, so I nudged Trude with my foot. She made a quick excuse of why we had to get home. My mind whirred, trying to work out who the mystery girls were. I didn't know anyone with hair like mine, and loads of people in Framton owned a bobble hat.

Chapter Fifteen

Mr Grainger was in the courtyard by his door when I went around the back of Gran's. Light spilled from the kitchen onto the uneven cobbles. He was giving the stones random little kicks and scrapes with his walking stick.

'Hi,' I said.

Mr Grainger looked up and gave me a small smile. 'Hello, Mallow. Good day at school?'

'It was okay. Um, what are you doing out here, Mr Grainger?'

'Tidying,' he said, gesturing at a tiny pile of weeds. 'Before Mrs Grainger gets back from the day centre. It'll cheer her up to see it shipshape.'

Poor Mr Grainger always looked so sad. Mrs Grainger had started wandering around the garden at night in her pyjamas. Sometimes she had a trowel in her hand as if she planned on doing some weeding. Other times she stood like a statue on the lawn.

'Need a hand?'

'No, dear. Nearly finished now.' He scuffed at a cobble with his foot. A piece of moss came away, which he shuffled into his pile. 'There, all done for today.' With a quick nod he hobbled inside, forgetting about the weeds. I picked them up and dumped them in the garden waste wheelie bin.

In the house Mum was leaning against the worktop by the kitchen window. She smiled when she saw me and flicked the switch on the kettle. 'Cuppa?'

I nodded and sat at the table, watching Mum as she made the tea. 'Where's Dad and Cal?'

'Cal's at Abraham's again. Dad popped to the DIY shop to pick up some parts. The dishwasher's still not working properly.' She carefully placed a steaming mug in front of me and sat opposite.

'I saw you with Mr Grainger.' Her hands circled her mug. 'Nice of you to make an effort. He's lonely, what with Lily being how she is.'

I shrugged. 'I feel sorry for him.'

Mum took a sip of tea. 'By the way, I've had a word

with Gran's doctors. She'll be coming out next week. Monday, they reckon.'

I pulled a face.

'Mallow, she can't help being old and sick. And she's going to be extra fragile now, so I'll need your support. This latest bout of pneumonia's knocked her for six.'

'Couldn't we find our own place nearby? Then you could still visit her every day.'

'Don't you like living here?'

'It's all right, I s'pose.' I picked at the skin around my thumb. 'If you like crematoriums.'

'Mallow,' said Mum. 'That's not a very nice thing to say.'

'Yeah, well, Gran's not exactly into the same things as me.'

'You and Gran don't know each other yet. Visiting for a couple of days a year isn't the same as being here all the time. And when we *did* visit you wanted to be with Trude rather than with Gran. And that was fine; Gran understood,' said Mum quickly, when I opened my mouth to argue. 'It just means you need to give it time; make a bit of an effort. Anyway, it wouldn't work us living somewhere else. Gran needs help at night and in the morning. I should be with her. And she's lonely here on her own since Gramps died; she doesn't have many friends.' She took another mouthful of tea. 'I understand it's been tricky living in her house, and getting used to a new school too, especially with what you've been through.' She stopped for a second and looked at me. 'But you and Gran have got more in common than you realise. In fact . . .' Mum hesitated. 'There's something she wants to talk to you about.'

I couldn't imagine why Gran wanted to talk to me. And what did I have in common with an old woman who liked living in a freezer and staring into space for hours? Wasn't she bored stiff? I decided not to say that aloud. Instead I slouched in the chair and crossed my arms, sticking my bottom lip out in a pout.

'I didn't want to leave my old life, Mallow,' said Mum suddenly. Her voice wobbled as she twirled the mug between her hands. 'I certainly didn't want to give up my job or our lovely home, *or* my friends in London. But Gran would have found it too upsetting to move from Framton, so it had to be this way.'

My mouth fell open. Mum had always acted as if the move was the most fantastic idea she'd ever had. Cheeriness had oozed out of her whenever she mentioned Framton, as if she couldn't wait to get here. And I'd been ecstatic to come; anything to get away from London. For the first time in ages I really looked at Mum: her grey roots, the bags under her eyes, the lines at the edges of her lips, her reddened knuckles from the hospital's anti-germ spray. Then I stared at my fingers, twisted around each other on my lap. 'Okay, I'll make an effort,' I mumbled.

Mum smiled. 'Thanks, love. Now, what news have you got?'

'Not much.' This would be the perfect moment to mention the messages and the photos. Mum had opened up to me, now it was my turn. But how could I add to her worry lines? And if I did, what good would it do? Being Mum, she'd want to speak to the teachers at school and then everyone would learn I was not only a blabbermouth, but a bald blabbermouth.

Mum let out a sigh. 'Well, I'm feeling fed up. It's been a long day. So . . . fancy helping me make some teacakes? That will cheer me up.'

Teacakes: yum. Especially Mum's ones. I grinned at her and took off my blazer. Mum switched on the radio and for the next half hour we measured and mixed and kneaded the dough while jigging around to the music, singing at the tops of our voices. By the time we'd popped the dough in a bowl and covered it in a tea towel to rise, we and the kitchen were dusted with flour.

'What a state,' said Mum, but she was giggling. She collapsed in a chair. She had a streak of flour along her cheek. 'Long time since we've done this, just the two of us.'

'It was fun,' I said, grinning at her. 'Can't wait to eat them. You could smuggle one into hospital for Gran too.'

'Good idea,' said Mum. 'She'd love that. She's missing home-cooked food.'

The smell of fresh dough wafted across the room. The kitchen felt warm, comfy and safe. For the first time in days I felt chilled out. All my worries had been pushed away.

Chapter Sixteen

It was just over a week to the Christmas ball. Everyone was discussing what they'd wear, and who was going with who. I wanted to join in, but the message creep was still OUT THERE. I couldn't relax.

By Thursday afternoon I was fed up with hearing everyone else's plans. It was a relief when the final lesson came – English, my favourite subject. Miss Reach asked us to write about an event in our lives that had changed us, which we'd then read out. Archie described how his house was burgled and said it had changed him because now he'd shoot the burglar. Faye's story was about when her cat, Fabiola, sneaked into the boot of the car and travelled to Wales with them. She didn't explain why that had changed her. I guessed she thought we'd be interested in her fabulous holiday at Plas Gogogoch Luxury Hotel and Spa.

Then it was my turn. I described a trip to Thorpe Park (before I lost my hair, obviously – rollercoasters being Number Three on my THINGS NOT TO DO list). How I rode on the maddest rollercoaster ever and threw up the burger I'd just eaten. The girl sitting on the ride next to me hooted with laughter until she realised she was covered in my sick. It had changed my life because I gave up eating burgers.

Everyone chuckled at my story even though I didn't mean it to be funny. *Today might not end badly after all*, I thought.

'And now,' said Miss Reach, 'announcement time. As you know, every year the English department chooses someone to give a short reading at the ball. The lucky person also gets a fantastic reward.'

I glanced at my watch – five minutes till the end of the lesson – snapped my book shut and slipped it into my bag. If I hurried, I could get home before Mum and have a cosy chat with Dad. Just him and me. I started collecting my pens together, only half-listening to Miss Reach.

'We considered all of you carefully but one person stood out . . . deserving winner . . . *mutter* . . . excellent work . . . flair for writing. This person is new to the school . . .'

New? My hand froze on the pencil case.

Miss Reach beamed. 'Well done, Mallow.'

'What . . . ?' A storm of clapping and whoops drowned my words.

Someone tapped my shoulder. I whirled around to see Dan's grinning face. 'Nice one.'

I opened my mouth to speak but I was cut off by the shrill ring of the bell.

'Right, off you go,' called Miss Reach, over the noise. 'And remember, the homework's for tomorrow! Mallow, come and have a quick word before you go home.'

I stood and picked up my bag as if on autopilot. People jostled past, calling out, 'Well done,' and, 'Cool!' but I was too stunned to reply. I used to love public speaking before I lost my hair – I even won a debating competition at my old school – but now the thought of standing on the stage, all eyes on me, made my skin crawl. I'd prefer to run around the gym ten times with a bucket on my head. My mind tossed over all sorts of hideous speech scenarios, each one crazier than the last. Like people turning up with bald head wigs and booing me. Or the creep invading the stage, and as everyone chanted, 'Off . . . Off . . . Off!' he'd rip the wig from my head.

While everyone else stampeded for the door, I hung

back, then hurried over to Miss Reach's desk.

'You should feel really proud, Mallow.' She smiled at me. 'There's not much time to prepare, but that'll stop you worrying. And I'm sure you'll cope well. It's up to you what your talk is on – you could read a passage from a favourite novel or a poem, or something you've written. And it needn't be long – five or ten minutes is plenty. The idea is to share something important to you with everyone. We reckon you're the perfect person to do the speech.'

'I don't want to,' I blurted.

'Oh,' said Miss Reach, looking a bit flustered. 'I'm sorry, Mallow, I assumed you'd be keen because you won that prize at your old school.'

I twisted my mouth into what I hoped was an apologetic smile. 'I am keen – I mean, I used to like public speaking but—'

'It's fine, I understand,' Miss Reach interrupted. Her neck had gone blotchy. 'My fault. I should have realised you might not want to get up on stage.' She looked at me with concern, and picked up the pile of books on the desk. 'But will you think it over for me, Mallow? Don't make a final decision yet. Perhaps talk it over at home and let me know? Then, if you still don't want to do it, we'll choose someone else.'

I nodded reluctantly and trudged out of the building. I'd made my mind up; there was no way I was going on that stage. I was so deep in my own thoughts, it took me a while to notice Dan loitering by the school gate.

'Hey.' He was leaning on the end of a new-looking, colourful skateboard. I found myself staring at it instead of looking at him. 'So, is that offer still open – to change at yours? Then we can go together?'

For a moment the words seemed to dance in the air between us. But the fearless, impulsive girl who'd made the spur-of-the-moment offer in the caravan had vanished. All that remained was the freaky, scared girl with the shiny secret under a wig. So, instead of saying, 'Yes, fantastic. I'd love to go with you,' what came out was: 'Uh, I'm not sure I'm going to the ball.'

Dan peeped at me through his messy fringe. 'What about the speech?'

'I'm not doing it.'

'Why not? Got to be worth it for the fifty quid or whatever they'll give you.' He had that baffled look on his face again. 'Has it got something to do with those messages you've been getting?'

I tried to think up a half-decent explanation without giving the real reason for not wanting to stand on the stage.

I stared at the tarmac path, then closed my eyes for a second – as if that would make the situation one iota better.

'Whatever.' He sounded so embarrassed. 'I'll sort something else out.' He dropped his skateboard on the ground and propped his foot on it. 'You know, I thought we'd got on well. At the caravan. Here's someone I can trust, I thought. I guess I was wrong. You don't want to go with *me*. That's the truth, isn't it?'

'No, wait . . . I mean, there *is* a reason I don't want to go, but it's nothing to do with you. I'd love to . . .' But Dan was on his skateboard, halfway down the road.

'Wait!' I called again, but he didn't look back.

*

Trude was waiting for me at the end of East End Road. She was deep in conversation with Beth.

'Beth says she'll help us set up a website for the business,' said Trude, grinning at me. 'Isn't that great?'

'I need to talk to you RIGHT NOW. In private,' I hissed in her ear, dragging her away from Beth. Then I started gabbling.

Trude grabbed my flapping arms. 'Slow down, hun. What do you mean, about the ball?' She wasn't in the same English set as me, but even so, I couldn't believe she hadn't heard the news.

After I'd explained, Trude gave me a sympathetic hug. 'I'm certain nothing bad would happen if you did the speech.'

'How can you be so sure?' I moaned. 'Anyway, there's something EVEN BIGGER I need to tell you.'

Trude was so excited by the news that Dan had asked me out, she didn't even question how a boy who'd barely spoken to me before was suddenly inviting me to the ball. Instead, she screamed and jumped up and down, only stopping when she noticed the look on my face. 'Don't tell me you said no?'

'Not exactly,' I said, and told her the rest of the conversation.

'Oh Mallow, you idiot,' she said.

'It's probably for the best. How can I go with Dan when I have this?' I tapped my head. 'It's impossible.'

'Hun, you've got alopecia, not two heads. Don't let it get in the way of you having fun. He doesn't want to go with your scalp; he wants to go with you.'

'But if he knew, he wouldn't.'

'Sort it out with him tomorrow.'

'I can't,' I said. 'Not now. It's too late.'

'No, it's not. Tell him you want to go with him.'

'You sound like my mum.'

'I'm only trying to help.'

'Yeah, well, don't. You're always trying to get me to 'fess up to my alopecia.'

'It's not like that,' said Trude.

'I'm starting to think you're the one sending me the messages. Forcing me to reveal my secret.' The words were out before I could stop them.

Trude gazed at me, her face suddenly as pale as paper. 'You don't mean that.'

'No, course not,' I muttered. 'But you've no idea what it's like being me.'

'No, I haven't,' said Trude, her brow furrowed into the deepest line. She turned away, then twisted round to face me once more. 'You've got to face facts, Mallow. You're missing out. You're in denial. You might never get your hair back, and then what will you do?'

I blinked. Apart from the GP, she was the first person to mention my hair not growing back. Not even Mum and Dad had raised that as a possibility – they were always upbeat and positive. And even though I realised deep down that there was a chance I'd have to live with no hair forever, I didn't want to admit it.

'Thanks for your support. At least I know where I stand,' I yelled as tears welled up. 'You know what?

You're obsessed with your stupid business ideas. You can find someone else to help you, because I'm not interested.'

I stomped off, cheeks blazing, squashing the niggle of guilt I had about my angry words. At the prom I glanced back but Trude had already turned away. What did she know? She didn't have to peer at a bald head every morning in the mirror. She didn't have to worry about strong winds, surprise photos, or make excuse after excuse why she couldn't go swimming or to a makeover party with friends. All she agonised over was whether to wear her hair up or down. Trude's hair worries and mine were poles apart. It was fine for her to say I should be having fun, but what if my secret was exposed on a stage in front of hundreds of people? In front of a boy I liked. However unlikely Trude thought it was, it could happen, couldn't it? Alopecia was my secret, and it was mine to keep. All the same, a picture popped into my head of a future me, sitting in a decrepit old house like Gran's, lonely and sad.

Chapter Seventeen

'Your turn, slowcoach,' said Cal.

Monday 5 p.m. and Mum and Dad had left to collect Gran from hospital, leaving me and Cal to enjoy the world's longest game of Monopoly in the drawing room. Cal's idea. I stared at the board. Life had got more complicated since I'd fallen out with Trude. We were steering clear of each other – no more walking to school together, no more lunchtime moanfests about lessons or the canteen food. No more messaging each other to share silly jokes. When I saw her chatting and laughing with Beth and Faye my insides clenched. Life was kind of lonely without her.

I caught Cal staring at me as I tossed the dice. 'What?'

'Why are you in such a sulk?'

'What's there to be happy about?' There was no way I was going to confide in my little brother what the real problem was. 'Gran's coming home. She's like a big, dark cloud hanging over the house.'

'Looked in the mirror lately?' said Cal. 'Your face is a big blob of gloom.'

I scowled at him.

'Gran's okay if you talk to her,' he said.

'Since when have *you* talked to her?' I moved my ship past Go and collected £200 from the bank.

'Loads of times. She's funny, and she's interested in my photos and told me about when she was at school.'

I was silent as I watched him race his car around the board and buy a hotel.

'It's not really about Gran, is it?' he said.

'Hmm?'

'The last time you acted like this you'd spent the night—'

'I don't want to talk about that.'

'Seriously, sis. You've been in a right mood for days now.'

'Cal, honestly, there's nothing else,' I lied. 'Come on, my turn. Hand over the dice.'

We heard keys jangling in the front door, and Gran's

voice from the hall: 'Stop fussing, Helen. I can do it myself.' The drawing room door creaked open and Gran appeared, taking tiny steps with the aid of a walking frame. She looked more shrunken and ancient than the last time I saw her. Her hair was a scraggy bird's nest and the skin on her neck was as crumpled as used tissue paper.

With a huff, Gran settled into the armchair beside the gas fire and peered at me and Cal. Mum and Dad scurried around, fixing cushions behind Gran's head while she wheezed and coughed, holding a screwed-up tissue to her mouth. Then she summoned me and Cal forwards to kiss her cheek. Her knobbly fingers clawed at mine, grasping them with alarming strength.

'Hello,' I murmured, trying not to flinch.

'Hope you've been looking after my house.' Her voice was like a rusty saw.

'Of course, Gran.'

'I told you there was no need to worry,' said Mum, busily rearranging flowers in a vase on the mantelpiece. 'We've taken good care of the place. Dave's even been working in the garden, haven't you?'

'I have.' Dad ran a finger around his collar. 'Everything's in order.'

Gran's grunt spluttered into a cough.

'Shall I get an extra cushion, Gran?' said Cal, springing into his 'aren't-I-a-fabulous-grandson' routine.

'Thank you, darling.'

Dad hurried out, muttering something about bringing stuff in from the car.

'Perhaps you should take a nap?' said Mum. 'You must be worn out.'

'All I've done in hospital is sleep,' said Gran, although she didn't object to Mum tucking a rug over her knees.

Mum beckoned me and Cal to leave the room and switched the main light off. 'Let's make some hot chocolate and then I'll start work on dinner.'

One hot chocolate and two biscuits later I was lurking outside the drawing room. My phone was in there; I could picture it on the coffee table next to the Monopoly game. It was a faint hope, but maybe Trude had messaged me? I eased the door open and peered into the dark room. The only light came from the fire. Gran seemed to be dozing – I could hear little snuffles and grunts. I inched my way towards the sofa, reaching out a hand, ready to grab my mobile without waking her.

'Is that you, Helen?'

I stopped moving. 'Only me, Gran,' I said. And then with my 'make an effort' promise to Mum ringing in my ears I added, 'How are you feeling?'

'Gasping,' said Gran. 'The tea was dishwater in that hospital. Make me a cup, will you?' *Cough. Cough. Splutter.*

I grabbed my mobile and hurried back to the kitchen.

'She wants a cup of tea,' I said.

'Bring my pills too, will you, Mallow?' Gran's squawk came from the sitting room. *Cough.*

Mum caught me rolling my eyes as she poured the tea. 'Don't be selfish, Mallow. You'd grumble too if you were in constant pain. And Gran's not used to having a house full of people. Can't be easy.'

'Things will settle down, poppet,' murmured Dad, as he squeezed past to take plates from the dresser.

'Yeah, when?' I grumbled.

Mum put the tea, a glass of water and two tiny pills into my hands. 'Here's the chance to do your bit. Go and chat to her.'

Still grumbling under my breath, I trudged back into the drawing room, glass in one hand, tea and tablets in the other. Gran had switched on the table lamp beside her and a warm glow now lit the corner of the room where she sat. It made her look a bit less deathly.

'Here you are, Gran, your medicine and tea,' I said,

placing the things on the table. 'Hot and fresh, just how you like it.'

'You needn't talk as if I'm a fool, Mallow. I might be sick but I haven't lost my marbles.'

'Right.'

'Come and sit here and talk to me.'

I sloped off to fetch the squishy leather footstool and plonked it next to the armchair. Gran swallowed the tablets with a sip of water and handed me the glass.

Minutes crawled by. Gran didn't speak. I was just about to start a conversation about the weather or ask if she wanted to play Monopoly when Gran piped up. 'Helen says you unearthed an old photo of mine.'

It took me a moment to register what she was talking about. Then I remembered the picture I'd found behind the radiator in Gran's bedroom. At last, a conversation topic.

'I'll get it!' I leapt up, ran to my room, dragged the memory box from under the bed and scooted back downstairs with the photo.

'Pass my specs, darling. On the side there.' I scanned the room and spotted them on the bookcase by the door. Gran perched them on the end of her nose and stared hard at the photo. 'Good grief, I remember Gramps taking this not long after your mother was born. Brings back memories.' Gran sighed and skimmed her thumb across the image. 'Oh, what a sight I am with that scarf on my head.' She glanced up at me over her glasses, reached out a hand and touched my wig. 'You've got such a pretty style. And the hair's much better quality than in my day.'

I stared blankly at Gran.

'I had alopecia too, when I was younger,' said Gran.

I blinked. 'What . . . ?'

'Close your mouth, Mallow. You look like a dying fish.'

'But why—?'

'Give me a chance and I'll tell you.' Gran picked up her tea from the table, her hand shaking so much the cup rattled in the saucer.

'I'll take that, Gran,' I said, removing the cup from her hand and placing it back on the table.

'Not as steady as I used to be,' said Gran, smiling weakly. She took a raspy breath. 'I was about the same age as you are now when my hair first fell out. And then over the next year it slowly grew back. And that was the pattern for the next thirty years; as soon as I had a full head of hair I'd lose it again.'

'Thirty years!' I couldn't disguise the dismay in my voice. 'It grew back though?'

'Eventually, yes. My hair's still thin if you look closely. But I didn't use any of these so-called treatments your mum insists on. Yours might grow back too. But in the meantime, it's best to get on with things.' As Gran peered at the photo again, I spotted a tear rolling down her cheek. She fumbled for her tissue and wiped it away. 'I never told anyone about the alopecia, apart from your gramps. Not even your mum knew, until the other day.'

I gawped at her. 'Why did you keep it from Mum?'

'Seems ridiculous now, but I was ashamed of my baldness, and it seemed easier to keep quiet. I didn't want your mum to be embarrassed by me. There didn't seem any point bringing it up. Until now, that is. I became an expert at hiding the bald patches. I always wore a wig and sometimes that scarf on top. As your mum grew up I was sure she'd notice, but she never did. As for other people, well, I didn't go out much.' Gran fingered a strand of my hair and sighed. 'This is gorgeous – so soft compared to the one I had.'

'You must have been lonely,' I said, thinking how different *I* felt from other people; how alone I was now I'd fallen out with Trude.

Gran made an odd noise, a cross between a harrumph and a yes. 'My life was cooking, cleaning and looking after your mum and Gramps,' she said and squinted at me. 'I know how grim it can be,' she continued, giving a wheezy cough. 'But keeping secrets can eat you up.'

'What would you have liked to do,' I asked. 'I mean, if things had been different?'

'Been a nurse; travel. And I loved dancing. When I had hair, Gramps used to take me to the local dances in the town hall. I'd get dolled up.' She leant her head back in the chair and closed her eyes, her chest heaving up and down as if the talking had worn her out. Then her eyelids quivered. 'It was my own silly fault – I should have done it all anyway, hair or not.'

I gazed at the photo in my hand. It didn't take much imagination to understand what life had been like with alopecia in those days. I opened my mouth to ask what she wanted me to do with the picture, but it looked as if she'd fallen asleep again – her mouth ajar, her right hand twitching on the arm of the chair.

Leaving her to doze, I made my way to my room. The memory box was where I'd left it on the bed, but the hinged lid was thrown back even though I was sure I'd shut it. I had a quick rifle through, but couldn't see anything missing. Cal, I fumed to myself. I took one last glance at the photo. Gran looked almost regal sitting in the grand armchair next to the fire, her legs and knees twisted to the side. An empty plate lay on her lap as if she'd had afternoon tea. And for the first time I noticed how miserable she looked. I guessed missing out on life did that to you.

As I was about to pop the picture back in my box I spotted something Cal had mentioned the other day. Framed in the large window behind young Gran was the garden with its green lawn and tall monkey puzzle tree. A long blob of grey – probably a squirrel, as Cal had said – obscured part of the scaly trunk. It looked out of place on the otherwise uniform brown tree trunk. It reminded me of something. But as soon as that thought entered my head, it flickered and vanished, like a puff of smoke on a breezy day.

Chapter Eighteen

Be there at 3.30 p.m. Or will reveal all.

The message was waiting when I woke up the next morning, sending a tremor through my body. It caught me off guard. It seemed like months since the last one, though it had been just a week. Stupidly, I'd actually started to believe my 'back off' message had worked. If only I'd blocked the number after all.

I wanted to call Trude, but thinking of her made my heart sink further. Would we ever be friends again?

I stared at the screen, waiting for the second message to arrive – the one with the photo clue of exactly where 'there' was. Five . . . ten . . . fifteen minutes later and I was still waiting.

The time ticked around to 8 a.m. I zipped the phone in

my bag and headed to the kitchen where Cal was busy slurping and crunching his way through a bowl of cornflakes.

'Where's Mum?' I asked as I popped bread into the toaster and grabbed the jam. The last thing I felt like doing was eating, but I figured I'd feel sicker with nothing in my stomach.

'With Gran, upstairs,' said Cal, peering out from behind a cereal box. 'Are you gonna puke? You're green.'

'No, I'm fine,' I snapped, but my tummy churned. Plain toast was all I'd be able to manage. I put the jam back in the cupboard.

My phone pinged again. I pulled it out. The image I'd been waiting for flashed onto the screen.

The shot was taken from a weird angle, as if the picture-taker was standing below and pointing the camera upwards. As my eyes adjusted to the scene, they focused on something grey, straggly and wig-like, hooked between what appeared to be two metal girders. I flipped back to the message and read through it again. Seven and a half hours to figure out where that photo had been taken.

'What's going on?' Cal had crept up behind me and was peering over my shoulder. '"Reveal all"? What does that mean?'

'Nothing,' I said, blanking the screen.

'Are you in trouble, sis? You keep looking at your phone as if it's a ticking bomb. What's up?'

I looked at his inquisitive face, with the sprinkling of freckles over his stubby nose. My gut told me to keep Cal out of it. The last thing I needed was him blabbing to Mum and Dad. On the other hand, I needed someone with a logical brain, good at interpreting photographs. If I could forget how annoying he was in an eleven-year-old brother 'I'm-so-clever' way, he could be my best shot at solving the sinister puzzle.

I kicked the door shut. 'First, you must promise not to tell anyone about what I'm going to show you.'

Cal raised an eyebrow. 'Okay.'

I gave him my phone and sank onto the chair next to his. He stared at the screen for a long, hard minute. 'What *is* this?'

'You tell me,' I said. 'It's somewhere in Framton.'

Cal peered at the screen again before looking back to me. 'Why do you want me to keep quiet?'

'Cal, are you going to help me or not?'

We peered at the picture together. 'Okay, so you want to know where this was taken. The trick is to look at the detail. The slightest thing can be a clue, even something you think is not important. Wait a sec.' He disappeared out of the room, returning moments later with Mum's laptop and a cable. He placed them on the table and tapped in Mum's password, flapping a hand at my questioning look. I watched as he connected my mobile to the laptop and tapped a few keys. He opened the pictures folder, bringing the photo up on the screen, enlarged but grainy.

'Hmm, doesn't help much – whoever took the picture isn't a photographer. See how blurred this is – they haven't tried to focus properly. Amateur.'

'Okay, okay, Mr Know-it-all,' I snapped. 'Can you tell what it is?'

'Could be a crane, or an electricity pylon. See the patches of sky in-between?' Cal took another look at the image. 'But there aren't any cranes in Framton and the nearest pylon is stuck in a field on Litchmore Farm. I've seen it on one of those mammoth walks Dad forces me to go on with him and Bilbo. The pylon makes a horrible buzzing.'

'Who'd climb a pylon and risk getting electrocuted?' I said, half to myself.

'What's going on?' Cal asked again, his eyes widening. 'This isn't like London, is it? The same thing's not happening again?'

'Of course not.' The half-lie made my heart wrench. I'd assumed Cal hadn't been too bothered by what happened before, that he'd shrugged the whole episode off. Maybe I'd been wrong. I gave him as bright a smile as I could manage. 'Stop worrying. Any other ideas of what it is?'

'Scaffolding? Plenty of that around here.'

We both squinted at the picture again. The metal bars were flat, not round like scaffolding poles. We were silent, lost in our own thoughts.

All of a sudden, Cal leapt to his feet. 'Got it! Framton Tower. Next to the crazy golf.'

Could that be it? The steel struts *were* angular and sharp like those on the tower. And it would explain the strange tilt, as if the photo-taker was standing far below. 'Cal, that's it!' I said, clutching him. 'You're brilliant.'

'Yep.' He gazed at me as he rubbed his arm. 'But why are you getting weird messages?'

'I can't tell you now, Cal, but I will, I promise. When this is over. Please don't let on to Mum and Dad.'

I wiggled my little finger, ready to link to his in a pinkie promise, a gesture we'd made since we were little.

'I've already promised,' he said, but his finger circled mine. 'Don't do anything stupid, will you?'

139

I forced a laugh. 'Course not. It's only a game.'

Cal stared at me – I could tell he didn't believe me. But then he shrugged and prattled on about how good he was at noticing things in photos, even old ones, like the one of Gran with the monkey puzzle tree.

'You'd better get to school,' I said, interrupting his ramble and pushing him into the hall. 'You don't want to be late.'

When the door had slammed behind him, I flung my books and pencil case into my school bag. Cal's jabbering about his skill at spotting things in photos got my brain ticking. Maybe I should have shown him the statue picture. Perhaps he'd have noticed something Trude and I had missed. Though we'd looked at the image until it had practically burnt holes in our retinas . . .

A sudden thought crossed my mind, and I darted into the hall and up the stairs. A murmur of voices was coming from the bathroom. Mum was still helping Gran get dressed. They'd be a while. Dad had taken Bilbo for a walk; he never got back before I left for school. I scooted into the kitchen and scrolled through the rest of my pictures on the laptop. First, the ones of me and Trude pulling faces at the camera. When things were normal between us.

Concentrate, I willed myself. Cal said to look at the detail. I took a deep breath as I clicked on the thumbnail picture of the rainy prom with the wig on the statue. Then I saw it. There *had* been something in that first picture. Something I'd dismissed at the time as a blur made by the bad light. If only I'd used the laptop before, instead of messing around with the tiny screen on my ancient mobile.

A blob of red jutted from the corner of the plinth. Out of place; a coloured smear in the grey picture.

I rubbed my sweaty palms on my skirt, then dragged my fingers outwards across the touch screen, closing in on the blotch. At first I zoomed in too much and the image blurred even more, so I inched out, little by little, until the shot came back into focus.

A foot – well, the toe of a red shoe – peeped from the base, as if its owner had hidden behind the statue while someone else took the photo. Somehow the fact that two people were involved made things worse. I peered closer, just making out lines running along the top. Laces? They were Converse All Star trainers. I was positive. The same as my ones in London, except mine were blue.

Suddenly I was back at Faye's, on the night of the sleepover. Ugly memories rewound in my head: the makeover, that silly film, scary Duke, Em and Faye

141

sprawled on the sofa with popcorn. And a pair of red trainers under the coffee table.

Faye and Em. One owned the trainers, the other took the photo. It made sense. The idea of them huddling together to hatch such a plan produced a nasty taste in my mouth. If I found those trainers, and they were the same as the ones in the photo, I'd know for sure they were responsible.

After saving a zoomed-in version of the photo, I inserted a sheet of paper into Mum's printer on the dresser and set it going. Seconds later the printer spewed out the paper. The picture was a bit grainy but it would have to do. I pocketed it and grabbed my school bag.

My mind was made up.

I was going to Faye's.

Chapter Nineteen

Ten minutes later I'd arrived outside Faye's house. I stood opposite and stared at the blank windows, my heart pounding. Part of me just wanted to creep away – I wasn't cut out for breaking into someone's house – but this had to end. Today.

I remembered Faye telling us once that her dad worked in London during the week. It was the one thing she and I had in common, what with my dad being away a lot too. The car wasn't in the drive – good. I hoped that meant her mum would be out for a while. Faye would have left for school already, so the coast should be clear.

With the street empty, I slipped through the gate leading to the back garden. A dog barked. How could I have forgotten Duke?

I rapped on the back door just in case Faye's mum, Laura, was still around. If so, I could make up a reason for being there. Duke howled from somewhere inside. I rattled the handle. Locked, as I expected. At home, Gran kept a spare key under a stone frog in the garden. Mum had told Cal and me about it when we'd first moved to Framton. It was a 'just-in-case' key, to use after school, if Mum got delayed. I was hoping Faye's family did the same. I scouted around. Two small terracotta plant pots stood either side of the back door. Too obvious a hiding place but worth a shot, I thought. I shifted the one on the left. It grated against the concrete path. Duke barked again.

Nothing.

I did the same with the one on the right. To my surprise, a key lay amongst the dirt and scurrying woodlice. I snatched it up, fumbling as I tried to fit it in the lock.

A minute later I entered the kitchen. I let out a sigh of relief – there was no sign of Duke, but whining and scratching came from behind the utility room door. A strong doggy smell mingled with Laura's pine incense sticks filled the air. I wanted to throw up.

With Duke out of the way, I crept through the kitchen and into the hallway. I paused, listening to the heavy silence of the empty house. It was weird being in someone's home without permission – it made me edgy. Had I committed a crime even though technically I hadn't broken in? Trespassing, I supposed. Whatever it was, I wanted to get out of there fast.

The family's shoes lined the skirting board in the hall. A quick glance told me that the Converse weren't there. They weren't in the hall cupboard either. I poked my head around the sitting room door. No luck there. The only other likely place downstairs was the utility room; I'd just have to assume Faye wouldn't put a new pair of trainers in with Duke. I hurried to the staircase. Faye's dad's binoculars were twisted around the bannister. After hesitating for a moment, I unhooked them and looped them round my neck. They might be handy when I went to the tower – I'd find a way to return them another day.

Faye's bedroom was still clutter-free. I opened her wardrobe. Three rows of neatly paired shoes lay at the bottom. No Converse. I grabbed the dressing table stool to reach the high shelf and found tidy piles of folded sweaters and tops. No shoes though. Nothing hidden under her bed, and her chest of drawers held no clues either. Was I searching the wrong house? If those red Converse weren't Faye's, they'd be Em's. I was on the verge of giving up and heading downstairs when I spotted Faye's laptop on the desk by the window. If I couldn't find the trainers, perhaps there was another clue waiting to be discovered. My fingers trembled as I tapped on the log in button. Locked. I typed in 'password'. No joy. Then her name, then 'Laura' and 'Duke'. None of those worked.

I looked around and saw the small photo of Faye's cat, lodged between the dressing table mirror and its frame. I typed 'Fabiola' into the computer. It worked. My hands shook as I clicked on the file of photos on her desktop and scrolled through them. There were plenty of close-up selfies of Faye and Trude together, a couple of Em, but none of the wig and none showing those red Converse.

I heard the scrunch of tyres on gravel. From the window I spied Laura's car pulling into the drive.

I froze.

A moment later came the scrape of a key in the lock.

THUD. The door slammed shut again.

I remained rooted to the spot.

CREAK from the stairs.

I closed the laptop and peered out of the window at the ground below. If I jumped I'd break a leg or worse.

How could I explain my presence in the house – in Faye's bedroom, alone – when I should be at school? Panic had turned my mind to mush. I'd just have to risk creeping down the stairs and out of the house and hope Laura didn't spot me.

My phone bleeped. The sound reverberated off the walls like a siren. Hurried footsteps came from the landing.

Laura entered.

'Faye? Oh, hello, Mallow.' Her surprised gaze flitted past mine as she searched the room for her daughter and then returned to me. 'Thought I heard a noise . . .' Her words tailed off in confusion. 'What are you doing here?'

'Uh, I popped by to pick up something.' I edged towards the landing and my freedom.

Laura's gaze shifted downwards. Too late I remembered the binoculars dangling round my neck. A clammy sweat broke out across my forehead as Laura's eyes widened. 'Sam's binoculars? Going bird-watching? Where's Faye?'

'She's left already,' I said, as I scooted past and belted down the stairs. 'Sorry, gotta go.'

'Wait a minute,' called Laura. 'What did you—?'

The end of the question was lost in the crash of me wrenching the front door open. As I dashed away, binoculars banging painfully against my chest, the sharp clip of Duke's claws on the tiled floor resounded behind me.

Chapter Twenty

The day dragged by so slowly I kept checking the clock to make sure the hands weren't travelling backwards. English, maths, history, art – each crawled by with me staring out of the window or nibbling my nails. When at last the bell rang I headed straight for the exit. Dan was hanging around with Fraser, but ignored me as I went past. Trude was standing in the corridor by the lockers with Faye. They were hooting with laughter at something, heads bent close together. As if they didn't have a trouble in the world. And I couldn't believe it: THEY WERE LINKING ARMS. I swallowed the lump in my throat, and battled my way through the crowds towards them. By the time I got there Faye had disappeared.

'Can I speak to you?' I asked Trude.

'What do you want?' she said, slamming the door of her locker. She didn't look at me as she stuffed some books into her bag.

'I shouldn't have said what I did. I'm sorry.'

'Okay,' said Trude, but she still didn't look at me.

'And I do want to help you with the business.'

'Are you sure?' said Trude, raising her head and meeting my gaze. 'Cos according to you I'm obsessed. You know, I had the idea that the business would help take your mind off things for a while. I thought it would help. And how could you even think I might be that message creep? That hurt, Mallow.' Before I had a chance to reply, she'd disappeared through the doors in a crush of Year Eights. I hadn't even been able to tell Trude about Faye and Em. I turned away, fighting back tears. It seemed I'd alienated everyone I liked.

Twenty minutes later I stood shivering at the foot of Framton Tower. From there I could see the beach stretching to the left and right. There was no one around; it was too cold, even for dog-walkers. A two-metre-high wooden fence surrounded the concrete base of the tower. Signs in big scarlet letters read 'DANGER. KEEP OUT.' and 'NO ENTRY', with scary drawings of a stick person falling off a collapsing building.

My phone pinged. Cal, again. He'd sent the message when I was in Faye's house too. It had said:

Don't do anything stupid. I'd been in such a panic I hadn't replied. It was too late anyway.

His new message said:

No answer? Where are you?

I tapped a response:

Don't stress. Home soon.

I dithered by the fence, wondering if Faye and Em were hiding somewhere. I hopped from one foot to the other, wishing my flimsy school shoes were fur-lined boots with thick soles. My breath floated in front of me before dissolving in the chilly air. I yanked my beanie further over my ears and tugged on my woollen gloves. The sky had turned steely grey and heavy clouds blotted out the wintery sunlight; it would be getting dark soon.

Where were they? The longer I stood at the bottom of the tower the bigger the ball of fury grew in my chest. I wasn't going to leave until I'd confronted them – forced them to admit what they'd done and got them to explain why. I focused Sam's binoculars on the steel, shifting the view one way, then the other. They almost slipped from my hands when I spied the wig dangling ten metres above me, fluttering in the breeze. My insides somersaulted. I twisted the button on the binoculars to focus more closely. Fingers of hair gave a come-and-get-me wave. The thought of passing it every day on my way to school was unbearable.

I grabbed the nearest fence panel and pulled myself up until I perched on the top edge. The tower loomed above me. I used the binoculars to see if Faye or Em was coming along the beach. There was no sign of either of them but there was someone at the far end of the prom. A boy with dark hair.

What was Dan doing there? I adjusted the binoculars, focusing on him. He could have been skateboarding, but I couldn't see his board. Or perhaps he was meeting Fraser and Archie. But I couldn't see them. Dan was leaning on the prom wall and seemed to be staring straight at me. Then he started to run towards the tower – towards me. Surely, I couldn't have been wrong about him? The binoculars clattered to the ground.

I jumped down onto the concrete at the foot of the tower. Panic was pushing me on. Bits of rubble and rubbish littered the ground. I circled the legs of the structure, looking for a ladder to climb. There wasn't one. Ignoring the cold, I pulled off my gloves and stuffed them in my pockets, then grasped the nearest strut. The icy sharpness of the steel bit into my palms. I hauled myself up and grabbed the next strut. A gust of wind picked up a loose electricity cable dotted with empty light-bulb sockets, whacking it against the steel in front of me.

I found a rhythm – foot here, hand there – until I was near the wig. It lay within reach. I stretched out my hand.

My fingers closed around the hair, but as I tugged, it snagged on a spike of metal. I jerked harder. The wig came free. I tucked it in the waistband of my skirt and took my first step towards the safety of the ground. But my foot got caught in a cable and it coiled python-like around my ankle. I tugged at it with one hand while gripping the frame with the other. My pump slipped off, vanishing into the murkiness at the base of the tower. Every time I moved my foot the cable tightened more. I was stuck.

Suddenly I couldn't breathe. My chest tightened as I was filled with a crushing panic. Blood pounded in my head and spots appeared in front of my eyes. I couldn't feel my fingers gripping the girders. My body was numb. I blew in and out, attempting to calm the drumming behind my ribs.

'Help!' The flex creaked as I adjusted my weight. Silence, apart from the wind whistling through the tower. No sign of Dan. No sign of Faye or Em. No one could hear me. I imagined the headline in the *Framton Gazette*:

'BALD GIRL DIES IN FAILED WIG RESCUE ATTEMPT'

And a picture of Mum, Dad, Cal and Gran sobbing over my open grave.

Then I heard someone call my name.

I wasn't alone.

Through my tears, I saw a dark shape coming for me.

Chapter Twenty-One

I screwed my eyes shut and gripped the steel, waiting for the end. Someone seized my hand.

I screamed.

'It's me, Mallow!'

I prised my eyelids open. Trude was perched on one of the cross girders, clutching the strut next to her.

'Trude, what are *you* doing here?' I panted, my head spinning.

'Come to rescue you, silly.'

We fumbled at the cable together, and somehow finally released my foot.

'But how did you know where I was?'

'Cal rang and told me about the message. He said he thought you might come here.' Trude shifted her weight on the beam. 'Let's get out of here. My bum's stuck to the metal.'

I gave a weak grin and got my shaky legs moving. Looking down made me dizzy. The tide was coming in, and now and then a trickle of water licked at the bottom of the platform of the tower. I concentrated on climbing down. A movement at the base of the tower flickered at the corner of my eye but then was gone. Seconds later we'd reached the safety of the ground and had climbed back over the fence.

I threw my arms around Trude. 'I'm so glad you came.'

'Listen, hun,' said Trude, 'I'm sorry about the other day. Us arguing is the worst thing.'

''S okay. I was being stupid. I never thought you'd sent me the messages. Ever. I don't know why I said that. And what I said about the business; I really do want to be a part of it. I'm sorry I've been so wrapped up in all this stuff.'

'It's okay,' said Trude. 'Mates again?'

'Yeah, course.' We gave each other a hug.

A scream came from the beach. Trude and I took one look at each other and stumbled down the steps to the shingle. Trude clutched my arm and I looked to where she was staring. Someone was on their back, where the concrete platform of the tower jutted onto the beach. As we got nearer, we saw Em stretched out on the shingle. She wasn't moving, her eyes were shut and her lips were purple. A wave rolled in and splashed her feet.

'Is she breathing?' said Trude.

I crouched to check. My toes curled as icy water slopped around them. 'Yes, but we need to move her.' We each took hold of an arm and pulled. We managed to drag her a metre or so but the shingle made it so hard we had to stop.

I glanced along the beach. In the dimness, I could make out a couple walking along the shore, but even though I shouted, they weren't near enough to hear me.

'She must have slipped off the platform. I'll phone for an ambulance,' said Trude, her voice trembling. She fiddled with her mobile. 'No signal. I'll run up to the prom and call from there.'

As Trude set off up the beach I sat beside Em. Her eyes flickered open, and she looked at me before giving a quiet moan. Her face was white, and there was a cut on her forehead. She struggled to sit up.

'Don't move. We're getting help.'

'I'm okay,' she mumbled.

'Yeah, right. You hit your head.'

The water licked at her legs. How long could an injured

person last in freezing water? My jaws clamped together with the chill.

A wave came, bigger than the rest. I gripped Em across her chest, trying to protect her as the iciness rushed over us. Seawater sprayed my face. The water drew back and the shifting shingle sucked at my feet and ankles, attempting to drag me into the sea. I still had Em under the arms. She made little gasping noises. My hands were numb and Em's body was heavy with water-logged clothes. My mind darted back to London, to another day. At least Em wasn't fighting me, like Sara had . . .

The sound of crunching shingle made me turn. Trude grabbed Em's arms. Faye was there too. She lifted Em's legs. Between the three of us we carried her away from the water's edge.

'You're gonna be all right,' said Faye to Em. 'The ambulance is coming.'

Em muttered something. I leant closer to her mouth.

'Thanks,' she said, her voice so faint I barely heard it.

Chapter Twenty-Two

We were sitting on a bench on the prom, wrapped in foil blankets: Trude, Faye and me. One of the paramedics had fetched us hot drinks from the café. We were waiting for a taxi to take us home. They'd whisked Em off to hospital to be checked over, but the paramedics said she should be okay. Two police officers had turned up too. They assumed Em had been messing about on the platform, slipped and banged her head. They quizzed us about what we'd been doing there. I wasn't sure they believed we'd just been passing by. They'd taken our names and details, in case they needed to speak to us later, and gone off to contact Em's parents.

My shoe was gone forever and the wig was no longer tucked in my waistband, probably lost on the beach or drifting out to sea. Not that it mattered now.

'So Em sent the messages?' said Trude, nursing her drink. 'I can't believe it.'

'It wasn't just Em,' I said, before Faye could open her mouth. I took the photo from my blazer pocket. Luckily, it was only a little damp around the edges.

Trude turned to Faye. 'But you wouldn't get mixed up in anything like that . . . would you, Faye?' Trude said, her voice catching.

Faye fixed her gaze on her steaming cup. The stress of the last few weeks bubbled up inside me and I rounded on her, thrusting the printout into her hand. 'You should have been more careful. Your trainers are in the shot.'

She stared at the picture. 'They're Em's.'

'Yours . . . Em's – same difference,' I stormed, getting into my stride. 'You took that photo, didn't you?'

Faye's face seemed to crumple in on itself. 'Yeah.'

'Faye!' said Trude. 'Why?'

'It started off as a joke; the wig on the statue looked funny.' When I heard the wobble in her voice I wasn't so sure she'd been having fun at all. 'It was supposed to be a one-off. Em promised it would end there, but things got out of hand.'

'And the other photos? This one? And this?' I thrust

159

the phone at Faye, swiping between the images from the golf course and the tower.

Faye's cheeks were pale. She twisted the cup in her hands. 'Em broke into the crazy golf course on her own.'

'But you came with her this morning.'

Faye nodded. 'I kept watch while she climbed up.'

'Once you'd lured me here, what were you going to do?' My heart was going a hundred beats a minute.

Faye looked down at her hands. 'I think Em was just trying to freak you out; she didn't have a real plan. She talked me into meeting her here after school. I wasn't going to come, but then I got worried about what might happen. I was late cos Mr Das Gupta wanted to see me. When I turned up I couldn't find Em; her phone went to voicemail. That's when I ran to the beach to wait and bumped into Trude. She told me what had happened.'

'Why should we believe your story?' Trude's cheeks were burning red, despite the freezing air. 'The whole thing might have been your idea.'

'I can't prove it wasn't my idea, but it wasn't,' said Faye, raising her gaze towards Trude, then me. 'I nearly told Mallow everything, but bottled it at the last minute. You remember, Mallow, at the statue that day? And I tried telling Em she'd gone too far, but she wouldn't listen.'

'You didn't try very hard,' I said, pulling the foil blanket over my head like a shawl. The wind had picked up again.

'Faye, how could you? You went along with everything,' said Trude. 'I thought we were friends. I thought we could *all* be friends.'

'We were . . . we are . . .' said Faye. 'But things changed when Mallow came. You didn't want to hang out any more. You were always rushing off to have lunch with Mallow or meeting her after school. Having Em as a friend was better than having nobody.' Faye took a deep breath. 'And I felt sorry for her. She didn't have anyone either.'

'I didn't know you felt like that.' Trude's chin wobbled. 'But the whole thing stinks. Mates don't do that to each other.'

'I'm sorry.'

It was weird how different people saw things in different ways. My mind was full of the times Faye had invited Trude for sleepovers and when they'd gone swimming at the leisure centre and shopping in town. Things I couldn't do. Little jealous thoughts had whizzed around inside my head. I hadn't seen things from Faye's point of view: how my friendship with Trude would affect her; how jealous she might have been.

'What did Em have against me?'

'She said you were a freak. That you didn't fit in. She wanted it to be just us three: me, Trude and her.' Faye's voice shook. 'And to be honest, I wanted the same. I thought we'd be better off without you around.'

'Oh, Faye,' said Trude, with a look of dismay.

'How did she find out about my alopecia?' I said faintly.

'Her cousin goes to your old school. She told Em everything.' So that explained Em's pointed little remarks at the non-sleepover.

'And what about Dan? I saw him here earlier.'

Faye threw me a guilty look. 'He had nothing to do with it. Em said it would be funny if you believed Dan was behind the messages. She knows you like him. She said it would clear the way for me and him to get together. I feel such an idiot for believing her.'

'So Em planted Dan's skateboard outside the crazy golf course,' said Trude, placing her cup on the ground at her feet.

'Hang on,' I said, flapping my hands. 'Did Em wear the wig at the café when you saw Dan? Lu said something about a girl looking like me.'

'Yeah, she wore the wig as a joke. Dan didn't recognise

her. Em's good at acting and she really did look different.' Faye covered her face with her hands. 'I never thought things would go so far. I should have stopped her.'

Before I could add anything, a car horn beeped and a taxi pulled up. I threw off the blanket and grabbed Trude's arm, hauling her up. Emotions walloped me from all sides: sadness, hurt, guilt, shock . . . since when had friendships become so tricky?

Faye stumbled to her feet too. 'Mallow, Trude, I'm sorry . . .'

Trude and I marched off. When I glanced back I saw Faye trailing after us, her head lowered. As we made our way towards the car, I caught Trude giving me sideways glances.

'What?'

'Your . . . um . . .' Trude gestured to my head. I reached up with my icy fingers. In the chaos my wig had shifted, dislodged by the breeze, seawater and foil blanket. A damp clump hung like seaweed down my left cheek, leaving bare scalp where the hair should have been. I fumbled, trying to pull it back, but the clammy mess slipped through my fingers.

As I clambered into the taxi a movement snagged my attention. Dan had appeared at the top of the steps leading to the beach.

Chapter Twenty-Three

'Is that you, Mallow?' called Mum from the kitchen as the front door shut behind me.

'Uh, yes.' My stomach lurched. I didn't want Mum to see me in a state. 'Off to get changed.'

'Come in here when you've finished, love.'

To avoid leaving telltale soggy footprints in the hallway, I slipped off my dripping tights and stuffed them and my remaining shoe in the understairs cupboard. Then I sprinted up the steps and grabbed a towel from the airing cupboard. My body screamed out for a steaming-hot bath, but Mum would wonder why I was having one in the middle of the afternoon. A super-quick shower would have to do.

Back in my room, I threw on the cosiest pair of jogging

pants and woolly jumper I could find. My thoughts kept returning to Dan. He hadn't been involved, that's what Faye had said. So why had he been running towards the tower? And had he recognised me when we were getting in the taxi? I let out a sigh. I didn't know why I was bothered by it. I'd already blown it with him. My mind switched to Faye – to what she and Em had done. I flopped on the bed. It was hard to understand how Em could hate me so much . . .

'Mallow! Are you all right up there?' Dad's voice came from the bottom of the stairs.

'Yep, coming now.' I took a moment to look in the mirror. My face looked pasty and pinched; my body felt weary. Would Mum and Dad notice anything? I hoped not. I didn't have the energy to explain right then.

On the way out of my bedroom, I caught sight of the wig on its stand on the dressing table. The hair was a nest of tangles and grey with dirt. I'd given it a quick wash but I would have to do it again later before the salt water ruined it. I took a deep breath, gave my scalp another wipe with the towel, and composed my face.

Dad was peeling potatoes at the sink and turned to smile at me. Mum was at the kitchen table with her laptop and a small bottle of pills. When I got nearer, I saw the treatment spreadsheet on the screen. A pink pill lay in a saucer on the table. Something inside me snapped.

'What's this?' I reached over and shoved the saucer harder than I'd intended. It clattered to the floor, the pill spinning towards the skirting board. Bilbo snuffled over and licked it.

'Drop, Bilbo!' Mum snapped. 'What *is* the matter, Mallow? It's just the next treatment. One pill before dinner.'

'I'm not doing it. THEY DON'T WORK.'

'But—'

'You never listen to what I want.'

'That's a bit unfair.'

'You're always too busy with Cal, or Gran, or your stupid laptop.'

'Mallow,' said Dad. 'That's no way to speak to your mother.'

As I stared at the hurt expression on Mum's face, Gran's rasping voice filtered in from the hall. 'What's wrong, Helen?'

'Nothing to worry about, Mum! Coming in a minute.'

'That's right, go to Gran, like you always do!' Then I froze.

Gran stood in the doorway with her walking frame.

'What's the shouting?'

'Just a little tiff, Mum. Let's get you sorted with that blanket.' Mum gave me her 'don't-think-you-can-get-away-with-behaving-like-that' glare and helped Gran from the room, leaving me and Dad staring at each other.

I could hear them muttering in the hall. 'Too much pressure . . . stop and listen . . . your daughter,' filtered through the open door.

'Mallow, don't be too hard on your mum.' Dad wiped a hand over his forehead. 'If I was around more—'

'But you're not.' I barged past Dad, shrugging off his attempt to stop me, and sprinted upstairs. The bathroom door handle punched a satisfyingly large hole in the wall as I flung it open. A chunk of plaster fell at my feet. I slammed and locked the door behind me.

Lined up on the shelf under the mirror were the remedies Mum had collected. All of them promised luxurious locks within weeks. In my mind I heard Mum's desperate words: 'One more try, Mallow. This might be the one.' I took an angry swipe at them. Jars, pots and bottles clattered onto the lino and into the bath. A plastic container burst and splodges of white cream puddled on the floor and splattered up the tiles. I crumpled onto the bathmat. Tears streamed down my face and snot dribbled from my nose. After a while I sat up, bum-shuffled over to the toilet, tore off some paper and wiped my nose and eyes. I'd spent over a year trying this and that medication, hoping for a cure. But none had worked for more than a few weeks.

There was a gentle tap on the door. Dad's normally cheerful voice sounded strained. 'All right, Mallow?'

'No,' I muttered.

'Mum's trying her best to help you.' I heard him shuffle on the landing.

Me: silence.

'What's wrong, poppet? Is this about the treatments, or is there something else?' He paused. Then, 'Why don't you open the door and we can have a proper chat?'

Me: silence.

'I wish I didn't have this blasted job miles away. I've let you down.'

'No, you haven't, Dad,' I whispered. 'But it's been so awful—'

There was the creak of floorboards as he padded away. He hadn't heard me.

Minutes later there was another knock. With soggy toilet paper balled in my fist, I scuffled over and pulled back the bolt. The anger drained from me at the sight of

Mum's face: wrinkled and blotchy as if she'd been crying too. She looked at the mess surrounding me, but didn't say a word. Instead, she perched on the side of the bath and watched as I splashed my face with water and dried it one of Gran's scratchy towels.

'I should have listened,' she said. 'Should have spent more time with you, less at the hospital.'

'I'm just sick of it.' I sat on the floor, my back against the side of the bath. 'My hair's gone and there's nothing anyone can do. I want to stop trying the treatments.'

'But there's this—'

I covered my ears with my hands. 'No, Mum. I mean it.'

For a moment the words hovered between us. I didn't dare look at Mum but the next minute I felt her warm body beside mine and her arm around my shoulders.

'Are you sure, love?' Her voice quivered as she gently tipped my face up and gazed at me.

I squinted through puffed-up lids and nodded. 'I mean, I'll never give up hoping . . . but I need a break.'

Mum's features relaxed as if the tension had been wiped away, and she squeezed me to her chest. 'I thought you wanted a cure so badly, I've been doing everything possible to find something that works. I wanted to see a smile on your face again – you've been so miserable . . .' Mum released me and blew her nose. 'Especially after what happened at your old school. Gran told me I was going too far; that the treatments weren't helping. I should have listened to her too.'

'I thought I'd be letting you down if I stopped trying,' I said, snivelling again. 'I want my hair back more than anything, but I need a life as well.'

'You could never let me down, love. I'm so proud of you.' Mum gulped and then chuckled. 'What a pair we are!' She picked up two tubes of cream and gave me a questioning look. 'You're certain?'

I took them from her and dropped them in the bathroom bin. 'Yep.'

One by one we chucked the rest in, each one clunking as it hit the bottom.

After we'd finished throwing all the tubes and bottles away, Dad suggested a takeaway. Nobody was in the mood to finish cooking dinner. While he dashed off to SuperFish, Mum and I sat drinking tea in the kitchen.

'I can't believe you didn't know about Gran's hair,' I said.

'A lot of things make sense now. Gramps gave me a camera for my birthday one year and Gran went ballistic.

170

I thought it was because she thought he'd spent too much money on it. Now I know she was worried I'd start taking snaps of her. She used to hide when I had friends to the house too. I wished she'd told me about her alopecia sooner. It might have helped her.' Mum sighed and gave me a small smile before taking a sip of tea. 'Oh, before I forget, Miss Reach rang to ask you something about the reading at the ball? I didn't know you'd been chosen!'

'Oh no, the speech!'

'Sounds like a great opportunity,' said Mum slowly.

'Mum!' I warned.

She held her hands up. 'Your decision – I won't mention it again. Just let Miss Reach know. She needs to make plans. There's someone else interested in taking your place.'

'Who?' It came out more sharply than I'd meant.

'Now, what was her name? I don't think you've mentioned her before.' Mum drummed her fingers on the table. My heart clattered against my ribs. *Thumpity-thump.* 'Elsie? Ella?'

'There is no Elsie or Ella, Mum,' I said, picking at the tag of skin around my thumb.

'Emily,' said Mum triumphantly.

Of course. Em figured she'd do the speech herself and

somehow reveal my secret at the same time. Or that's what she thought. But maybe she wouldn't get the chance.

I slipped out of the kitchen, asking Mum to let me know when Dad came back with the takeaway. I was so tired I could barely clamber up the stairs. In their own ways, Gran, Trude, Miss Reach, Mum and even Em had all been trying to tell me the same thing.

Hair or no hair, I needed to be ME.

Chapter Twenty-Four

'Hold still, hun, while I stick the last one on.' Trude hadn't batted an eyelid when I'd taken my wig off in front of her for the first time. She'd simply sat me down and got to work. Two hours later, she'd almost finished.

'There.' She swivelled the chair around till I faced the mirror and finally I could see what she'd done. I gasped. Mum had helped me shave off the remaining wisps of hair, and Trude had covered my scalp with tiny pink, lilac and yellow gems, to create a trumpet-shaped flower over my head – my namesake, the mallow. A sparkly green stem and leaves curled around the back of my scalp, down the sides towards my ears and to the nape of my neck. Trude had used special paints to fill in the gaps between the gems. It was like a stunning, glittery, skin-tight cap.

'Where did you get these beads?' I'd never seen anything so lovely. My fingers skimmed over the gems, mesmerised by the elaborate design Trude had created.

'Online. I've had them for months, hoping one day you'd let me have a go,' said Trude, her cheeks going pink. 'Have I done all right?'

'It's beautiful,' I said, twisting left and right to admire my profile. 'You're amazing.'

'Glad you like it.' Trude smiled at me. 'You look gorgeous.'

'Trude.' I turned to face her, taking her hands in mine. 'I don't know what I'd do without you. You've stuck with me all this time. I hated it when we fell out. Nothing felt right. It was as if my life was falling apart.'

'I hated it too. Mum threatened to send me to boarding school so she wouldn't have to put up with my miserable face.' Trude grinned at me. 'Let's never argue again.'

'Agreed,' I said, and we hugged each other.

We spent ages getting ready. My simple, pale-green dress, which Mum had given me as a surprise, went so well with the shimmering head beads. Trude had an elegant pink, floor-length gown with thin diamante shoulder straps and lacing down the back. She'd plaited her hair and twisted it on top of her head like a crown.

While I was twirling in front of the full-length mirror in Mum and Dad's room, there was a tap at the door. Cal came in, his hand scrunched into a tight fist.

'Here,' he said. He opened his fingers to reveal Gran's dragon clip. 'Sorry.'

'My clip, you stole it!' I gasped, recalling the day I'd found my memory box open on the bed. I'd forgotten to tackle Cal about it. 'What were you doing with it?'

'Don't stress. I only took it to show Mr Grainger. If I'd asked, you wouldn't have let me. Anyway, he used to work in antiques. He says it's worth at least three hundred pounds! I thought it might help with paying for treatments. Guess we're not going to the States now though?'

I grinned and shook my head. 'Thanks, Cal, but I won't sell it, not even for a trip to the States.'

He shrugged. 'Worth a try. Hey, I like your head. Shame about your face.' The pot of hand cream narrowly missed him as he scuttled from the room.

'Ooh,' said Trude, when she saw the clip. 'That will go so well with your dress.' She fastened it onto the shoulder strap of my outfit. The gleaming red eye of the dragon twinkled and flashed. 'Looks just as good as it would in your hair.'

No posh limo and chauffeur for us. Just Dad in his old

Volvo. I didn't care; I was too busy quashing the panic in my chest. By the time we arrived at school there were just a few stragglers in the car park. Most people had disappeared inside the hall. Goosebumps peppered my body as I got out of the car, and I was glad of the little hooded shrug Mum had lent me. I was about to ask Trude if she'd spotted Dan when Miss Reach hurried over.

'We're opening the ball with your speech, Mallow. Are you ready to go in?'

My whole body was trembling, but I managed to nod and Trude opened the double doors.

The hall had been transformed. Glitter balls hung from the ceiling, silver balloons were taped to the walls and blue streamers had been draped over the beams. With the lights dimmed I could almost imagine we were in a proper ballroom (apart from the plastic chairs and trestle tables holding bowls of crisps and non-alcoholic punch). A blue banner was slung above the stage, saying: 'Welcome to the Year Nine Charity Christmas Ball'. The hall was stuffy and warm. I pulled my shrug off and placed it on a free chair. A bead of sweat trickled down my temple as I turned towards the stage.

As we pushed our way through the crowd there was a shared gasp, and whispers travelled around the hall. A hundred pairs of eyes drilled into my back as, cheeks burning, I wound my way towards the stage. Trude was by my side, her arm looped through mine. The mutterings got louder and I concentrated on putting one foot in front of the other. I tried to drown out the murmuring voices by humming under my breath.

The walk to the stage lasted forever. But finally we were at the steps.

I can do this, I repeated in my head, over and over again. *I can do this.*

Miss Reach smiled at me and gave my arm a quick squeeze. Somehow I got my jelly legs to climb the steps. The other teachers were sitting at the back of the stage. Mr Das Gupta caught my eye and stuck both his thumbs up. I gave a nervous smile back, took a deep breath and turned to face the crowd.

For an instant, as I gazed out at the sea of faces, I wanted to run away. But then I clocked Trude standing at the front, next to Fraser and Archie. She grinned and shook her phone in the air, ready to take a snapshot. I gave a little wave. My eyes panned across the hall. Faye was standing on her own near the door to the toilets, looking miserable. I carried on searching for the one person I both half-dreaded yet half-wanted to see.

But he was nowhere.

As Miss Reach took her place in front of the microphone, a tingling heat spread over my decorated scalp. I prayed the beads would stay stuck. 'Welcome to the annual charity Christmas ball in support of the Wishing Well Children's Fund,' Miss Reach began. 'I'm delighted Mallow is giving what has become a tradition at Framton Academy – the Year Nine speech. She is doing something very brave – she is going to talk about what it's like to live with alopecia. Anyway, she'll be able to explain it much better than I can, so I'll hand over to Mallow.'

No turning back now. I stepped in front of the mic. My hand shook as I twisted the stand to lower it to the right height. I hadn't written my speech down. For a second, my mind blanked. *Calm down*, I told myself. I took a shaky breath and started to speak.

'I know what you're thinking, but I'm not ill. I don't have cancer and I'm not about to die. I have an autoimmune condition called alopecia areata. My wonky immune system has gone berserk and is attacking my hair follicles. Don't worry; you can't catch it from me.

'My hair fell out without warning. There was no "By the way, Mallow, you'll wake up tomorrow with a lot less hair than you went to bed with." There was just a handful of wispy blonde strands on my pillow. And the next morning, and the next. It's not painful, though my scalp can get itchy sometimes. I can do the same things you can. Inside I'm the same as you, but I look different. The doctors can't say when or if my hair will grow back. If it does, it might fall out again.' I stopped and took a deep breath. 'There is no cure.

'It was a massive shock for me and my family. I've found it hard to tell people about it – it's old men who go bald, not fourteen-year-old girls. It's taken a long time to accept that this is how I am. It's not easy to walk in a hairy world and believe that bald is beautiful. Without the support of my family and friends I don't know where I'd be.'

My voice cracked, and I stopped for a moment to swallow, my mouth dry. Miss Reach handed me a tumbler of water and I took a grateful sip. Then I began again.

'My dad tells me we're all different. He says going bald could happen to anyone. I just wish it hadn't happened to me. But I'm learning to live with it. So, do me a favour. Don't whisper or snigger. Don't stare at people who look different. Don't call us names. If you've got a question, come and ask me straight. I'm just like you. I've got hopes, dreams and ambitions, and having no hair makes me more determined to achieve them.'

There was silence when I finished. Then the clapping started from the back of the stage. I twisted round to see Mr Das Gupta and all the other teachers on their feet. That set everyone else off and soon cheers and whoops reverberated off the walls. The next thing I knew, Miss Reach was presenting me with my prize: a fifty-pound gift voucher. She had tears in her eyes, and so did I.

Chapter Twenty-Five

I left the stage and stumbled down the steps. Trude stood at the bottom, ready to give me a hug. And then everyone – Trude, Archie, Fraser and Beth – crowded around, thumping me on the back and smiling as if I'd just won an Oscar. The school band started playing and suddenly everybody was dancing.

'Where's Dan?' I shouted in Trude's ear.

'Dunno,' Trude shouted back. 'Haven't seen him.'

My insides twisted. Of course, why would he come to hear me speak after I'd blown him out like that? The adrenaline from the speech fizzed away as quickly as it'd appeared. I told Trude I needed some fresh air.

'Want me to come too, hun?' she asked.

I shook my head. 'Nah, Archie's waiting for you.' My

gaze slipped to where Archie stood, leaning against the wall by the table. I couldn't help noticing his laser stare in our direction.

'We're just friends.' Her cheeks reddened.

'If you say so . . .' With a grin, I gave her a gentle push towards him.

Huddled in Mum's warm, fluffy shrug, I left the building and tottered down East End Road. The sounds from the school hall faded, replaced by seagull shrieks as I reached the promenade. I abandoned my strappy sandals by the prom wall and headed onto the beach. Sharp stones and rough pebbles dug into the soles of my feet. The glow from the street lamps filtered onto the shingle, and I sat down, hugging my knees and gazing into the blackness. The soft rush of waves was soothing and the breeze had dropped. In the distance, the lights of an oil tanker twinkled in the murkiness.

The scrunch of stones and pebbles startled me and I glanced up to see Dan. He looked uncomfortable in a black jacket. He'd undone the top button of his shirt and a loose tie flapped around his neck.

'Hi,' he said.

'Hi.' My heart thumped.

'Trude told me about what the messages said, and the

photos. It must have been tough . . .'

'It's okay now,' I mumbled, my gaze boring into the darkness.

'If I'd known it was you up the tower I'd have run faster.'

'What?'

'I saw someone climbing but I didn't know who it was.'

'You were running to help?' Happiness bloomed in my chest.

'Yeah, but by the time I got there I couldn't see anyone. I hung around a bit to make sure, but stupidly I didn't check the beach. Then the ambulance and police arrived. They wouldn't let me anywhere near you lot. The next thing I saw was Em being carted off in the ambulance.' He let out a breath and glanced down at me. 'By the way, your head looks incredible.'

'Thanks. That's Trude,' I said, reaching my hand to my scalp. 'She did it all.'

'Great speech too. You did a brave thing.'

'You were there?' I was glad the darkness meant he couldn't see my blushes.

'Course.'

He sat on the pebbles and glanced sideways at me. 'Is

your alopecia why you didn't want to go to the ball with me?'

'Kind of.'

'Should have guessed something was up,' he said. 'I don't care about your hair, you know. Doesn't matter to me.' He stared at his hands. 'It's you I like.'

My heart flipped. 'Me too. I mean, you're not bad yourself.' *Could I have made myself sound a bigger idiot?*

'Thanks.' Dan gave a shy grin and then shook his head. 'What Em and Faye did . . . unbelievable.'

I swallowed hard and folded my arms tightly across my chest. 'It's not the first time.'

Dan looked at me. 'What do you mean?'

'Being bullied; it's not the first time.' I cast a sideways glance at him. Maybe here in the dark, on the beach, with no one else in sight, the moment had come to take the plunge. 'Want to hear about my worst Bad Hair Day ever?'

Dan raised an eyebrow. 'Go on.'

'I skipped school. It was when we lived in London.'

'Because of the bullying?'

'Yeah. We had swimming first lesson on a Friday. Since my hair loss I always sat on the side – I was worried my wig would fall off in the water,' I said as an explanation, though Dan hadn't asked for one. 'Things had become terrible at school. There was this girl, Sara. She used to be my friend, but when I lost my hair, she wouldn't be seen with me. Said I was bad for her image. She ganged up with some other girls. They called me names, laughed at me. Sometimes . . . sometimes I caught myself wishing I really *was* ill cos I didn't think they'd dare pick on me then.'

Dan was quiet. The only sounds were the whoosh of the sea and the far-off wail of a siren.

'That Friday, Sara went too far. The class were lined up ready for the start of the lesson. I was sitting on a bench, as usual. The teacher had gone into the little office to fetch something. Then Sara pulled my wig off and threw it in the pool. Everyone laughed and pointed.'

I paused and scrunched my eyes shut, picturing the scene again. The memory felt as sharp and as raw as if it had happened yesterday. I could even smell the bitter chlorine from the water, hear the cackles of laughter as everyone watched my wig floating like seaweed into the middle of the pool.

'I was so embarrassed. I wanted to be anywhere but there. Sara was standing at the edge of the pool and put a foot out to trip me as I ran past. I managed to dodge her, but I slipped. As I fell, I grabbed her arm – it was a reflex reaction to stop myself falling in. We both ended up in the deep end.'

'She deserved it,' said Dan with a snort.

'She could barely swim.'

Dan went quiet. Then he said, 'So what happened?'

'Her friends were hysterical – shouting and shrieking. Sara panicked, trying to swim to the side, but she kept going under. I moved to grab her . . .'

I remembered the weight of my saturated clothes, and how Sara thrashed and kicked and screamed as I'd struggled to tug her to the edge. How in her panic she'd pushed my head so it had gone under and my mouth had filled with water. How her nails had clawed at my arms as I'd tried to remember the life-saving tips from the swimming lessons I'd had before I'd lost my hair. How I'd thought we'd both drown.

'Two other girls jumped in, and then the teacher. We managed to drag Sara to the side. Her skin had gone blue, her breath was raspy . . .' I stopped, lost for a moment in the awful memory. 'Her friends kept screaming at me that I'd killed her. I didn't know what to do, what to say—'

'Was she . . .' Dan paused. 'Was she okay?'

'I . . . didn't wait to find out.' A lump rose in my throat. I pressed my curled fingers against my eyelids. The heels of my palms mushed against my lips. When I spoke, my voice was muffled. 'I was desperate to . . .'

'What?' Dan gently prised my hands away from my face but I didn't meet his eyes.

'To get away. Escape. So, I legged it.'

I'd gone into the cloakroom and changed into my tracksuit, and put on my beanie to cover my bare scalp. I knew it was the wrong way to handle things, that running away wouldn't help, but I wasn't thinking straight. It seemed the only thing to do.

'Where did you go?'

'Wandered round the shops. At that moment I hated school, my life, everybody. I wanted to leave it all behind.'

The day had been awful – it had rained constantly and by the end of it I was cold, wet and even more miserable. I ended up at the train station, thinking I'd visit Trude, but I didn't have enough money. When it got dark, I'd found a café that stayed open late and sat there with a mug of tea. I only left when the café owner chucked me out.

And worse was to come. The school head rang Mum and Dad – Dad was on leave – and told them what had happened; that I'd gone missing from school.

'I'd turned my mobile off to stop Sara's mates hassling me, which meant Mum couldn't reach me either. In the end

I had to go home. There was nothing else to do, nowhere to go. It was 1 a.m. or something. I'd been missing since around nine that morning. Dad had called the police and Mum and Dad's friends had organised a search party. The neighbours got involved and everything. I'd never done anything like that before. Never got into trouble, never run away.' My cheeks burnt from the memory. 'They spent hours worrying and searching for me.'

'But your family must have been so relieved when you turned up at home.' Dan shifted next to me. I could feel the warmth of his body.

'Yeah,' I said in a small voice, remembering the look on Dad's crumpled face before he realised I was standing in the doorway to the kitchen. And me staring in confusion at Dad, then at Mum, and finally at the two fed-up-looking police officers sitting at the table with untouched mugs of tea. Somehow I thought my parents wouldn't care if I was missing. I was wrong. Mum and Dad made me promise never to run away again.

'What about Sara?'

'Mum told me she was treated for shock and sent home, thank god. But the whole thing was a nightmare.' My eyes prickled.

'It must have been hard, back at school.'

188

'I didn't go back,' I mumbled, staring down at my lap. 'It was only a few weeks till the end of summer term. The head gave me a temporary exclusion, even though it wasn't my fault. Sara was given one too. The head said she needed to take a hard line because of how dangerous the situation was. She said we shouldn't have been messing around by the pool; that I shouldn't have left the school grounds afterwards. She said the suspension would give me a chance to get my head together. Three weeks later, Mum and Dad announced we were moving here to look after Gran.'

'Rough.'

'Yeah. And the worry I caused. Mum and Dad—'

'Bet they didn't blame you.'

'No, they didn't.' Mum and Dad weren't even angry. I remembered Dad leaping to his feet and hugging me so hard it took my breath away. Mum and Cal crowded round and everyone had cried and laughed at the same time. It had been pretty humiliating having to face my family and the neighbours who'd formed a search party, and explaining to the police where I'd been and why. And the headline splashed the next day on the local newspaper's website and Facebook page for everybody to see:

'Bullied Bald Girl Back Home Safe and Well'

'So that's why you wanted to keep your alopecia a secret?'

I nodded. 'I was fed up with it – so tired of everyone knowing, the bullying, being treated like a freak. I wanted to make a fresh start here, where no one except Trude knew about my hair. It hasn't worked out though. I should have known that keeping it a secret would be impossible. And Mum and Dad have treated me differently since then. Dad feels guilty for leaving us every time he goes back to the rig. And Mum . . . well, Mum thinks everything will be fixed if she finds a treatment that actually works.'

Everything was shifting and changing around me. I'd dropped the pretence of having hair. I'd told Mum I didn't want to try any more treatments. And now I'd told Dan what had happened in London. The weight on my shoulders had turned into dandelion seeds.

'Hey, I've got to thank you for something,' said Dan suddenly.

'What?' I asked, tugging my shrug further around my shoulders.

'You said it was cool the way me and Dad lived. So I went for it – I told Fraser and Archie about the caravan. I figured if they didn't like it then that was their problem. Anyway, they were fine – stunned I hadn't told them before – but fine. They've even been over. Played footie in the field.'

'That's fantastic!'

'Yeah, I´ve been lucky. Wish things had been as simple for you.'

I got to my feet and turned to look at him. And in that moment, seeing Dan sitting on the shingle, with his serious chocolate eyes, his lips twitching into a shy smile as he gazed up at me, I took a risk. 'I've probably blown it . . .' I began, touching my scalp. 'But we could go out . . . if you'd still like to, that is?'

'That'd be cool,' he said straightaway. He leapt to his feet and held out his hand. 'Want to walk back?'

I grinned as his warm fingers circled mine.

Leaving the dark shore behind, we headed back towards the warm glow of the promenade.

Chapter Twenty-Six

I was heaving the chest of drawers into the middle of the bedroom, ready for the decorators, when there was a gentle tap at the door.

'Can I come in?' Gran was standing in the doorway, huffing from the effort of climbing the stairs.

'Course.' I stood back to let her in.

'I expect you're looking forward to getting this room decorated,' said Gran, as she sat on the end of the cluttered bed. 'It'll feel more like your home then.'

'Mum said this used to be her room when she was young.'

'Yes, for a while, until she persuaded me to let her have the big bedroom at the front of the house.' Gran's gaze swept across the threadbare carpet, chipped paintwork and shabby curtains. Dark, tacky spots peppered the wall where I'd removed the photos of Mum, Dad, Cal and Trude, and the most recent one of me dressed for the ball (the first picture I'd let anyone take of me for months). Everything was tidied away into my memory box for now.

'I should have decorated in here long ago,' said Gran. 'Still, now you can make it the colour and style you want.' She clocked my new collection of wigs on their stands and smiled. 'A bit like your hair.' I was getting used to being bald, but I still liked having hair on my head. It was so cold without it, especially now it was January. Besides, there was the problem of meeting people for the first time. Having to explain what was wrong with me. That would never go away. Still, it was fun turning up at school with brown hair one day and blonde hair the next.

'I'm glad you're finding a way to deal with your hair loss, Mallow. Things will get easier, although it might not feel like that right now. Your mum and dad are so proud of the way you're coping. You're handling it much better than I did.'

I looked down at my hands and blushed. 'Dad's off again tomorrow. I'll miss him loads.'

'I'm sure you will, but he'll be less worried about you this time. And how was yesterday's shopping trip with your mum?'

'It was good. We got some stationery for when my desk arrives from London.'

'And binoculars?' Gran raised her eyebrows as she picked up the box containing the new pair I'd bought to replace the ones belonging to Faye's dad. When I'd gone back to find them at the tower, the lenses had been cracked and I'd had to bin them.

'It's a long story,' I mumbled, feeling my cheeks warm.

'Save it for another day,' said Gran. 'Or perhaps it's best I don't know.'

I grinned. 'I told Mum I wanted to do other stuff with her – besides visits to the doctor's and searching for new treatments.' I looked at Gran. 'You talked to her about that too, didn't you?'

'Pah, I did nothing. It's been down to you, darling.' Gran straightened her back and placed her hands on her knees. 'Are things better between the two of you now?'

I nodded, swallowing the lump in my throat. 'Yeah. I think so.'

'That's good. And if you need to talk, you know where to find me. Speaking of which, I'd better start my packing.'

'Do you mind moving into the stables?' I asked.

'Darling, it was my idea, as soon as I learnt the Graingers were moving to those new flats in town. I've been thinking about getting a smaller place since I came out of hospital. The stables will suit me fine. Your mum will be on hand to help when I need it, but it means I've still got my own space. And you've got your space too. This house needs a family living in it.' She got to her feet. 'It'll take some adjusting, but we've all got to do that, haven't we?'

Mum's head poked round the door. 'Ah, there you are. I've been calling and calling. Didn't you hear me?'

'We were having a nice little chat,' said Gran, winking at me.

'We have to get on,' said Mum, 'if you want your things moved over to the stables tomorrow, Mum. Or we could always leave it for a bit.'

'I'll be fine, Helen. Stop fretting,' said Gran. 'You'll only be across the courtyard. Hardly Australia, is it?'

Mum took a deep breath. 'You're right. Old habits . . .' She broke off as she handed me a glossy leaflet. 'Mallow, here's something to read.'

I groaned. 'Mum.'

'Don't worry,' said Mum. 'Just have a look. No pressure or anything.'

She and Gran left me to it. I sat on my bed and scanned the leaflet headed 'Alopecia Summer Camp, Scarborough.' It was about a charity that arranges a short holiday each year for sufferers of alopecia and their families. It looked kind of fun, and it meant I'd meet others like me. Maybe not as exciting as the States, but I could live with that.

My mobile rang. I rummaged under my duvet and pulled out the super-sleek new gold phone Mum and Dad had bought me for Christmas.

'Are you coming over, hun?' asked Trude.

'Yep, give me a few minutes to finish here,' I said.

'Have you come up with a name for my online business yet?'

'What about Beads for Baldies?'

'Brilliant – I love it!' said Trude. 'I knew you'd be good at this. The next thing I need is a model for the designs. I could use one of those mannequin heads, but it would be much better on a real one—'

'No way,' I interrupted. 'I don't want my scalp plastered all over the internet.'

'Please, please, please,' said Trude. 'I won't show your face, I promise. We could do demonstrations on YouTube as well. I'll make you design consultant. Then you can have a say in what I do.'

It was great to hear Trude so excited about her new idea: selling the sorts of beads and paints that she used on my head for the ball. 'Okay, but on one condition.'

'What's that?'

'You let Faye help with the business too.'

Trude snorted. 'She doesn't deserve it, hun. Not after the way she treated you.'

'She's changed,' I said. 'I think she really is sorry. She's been defending me when anyone at school asks me tricky questions about my alopecia. The last thing I want is for someone else to be miserable.'

Trude huffed. 'I suppose it would be nice to all be friends. And with Em gone, Faye must be extra lonely.'

I wouldn't miss Em AT ALL. In the end I'd told Miss Reach about the bullying and the school gave Em a temporary exclusion. But she didn't come back after that. Maybe she just couldn't handle facing me every day. Dan and I had spotted her walking along the High Street in Fossilworth last week. She had a posh new uniform on from one of the private schools. If she saw us, she pretended not to. But a couple of days later a note was posted through our letterbox. It just said 'Sorry.' Maybe what happened at the tower had made her think. Maybe.

None of it mattered now. As Dan said, if Em couldn't

accept me as I was, that was her problem, not mine.

'Gotta go, Trude,' I said, as I peered out the window and gave a wave. 'Dan's here. We'll see you in five.'

'Say hi to lover boy for me,' said Trude.

'He's not lover boy. Anyway, you can tell him yourself.'

'Only joking,' said Trude. 'I want to quiz him about running a business. He might have picked up stuff from his dad. And yes, before you say anything, I'll message Faye and ask her to come too. There's so much to do.' I heard her give a happy hum as I hung up.

'Mallow?' called Dan from the bottom of the stairs.

'With you in a sec!'

I picked up the new binoculars for Faye's dad and took one last look around my room. A slant of sunlight fell on the worn carpet and tiny specks of dust danced in the air. It was difficult to remember the insecure girl who'd moved here in September, who'd wanted to hide under the duvet and never come out. I smiled to myself as I headed downstairs. Mum told me that all I needed was to get my confidence back. She said that if I had confidence, I could cope with anything.

Now at last I'd found it.

THINGS TO DO:

1. *Help Trude start the online business.*

2. *Swim in the sea.*

3. *Enter school debating competition.*

4. *Have a sleepover.*

5. *Be me!*

Post a review!

Let me know what you thought of ***Bad Hair Days*** by visiting **jm-forster.co.uk** and filling in the contact form or by posting a review with your favourite online retailer. You can also join my mailing list on my website to keep up-to-date with my news.

Acknowledgements

To my online writer friends at WriteWords for providing top-notch critique and support. Without you I wouldn't be a writer. To Book Frisbees for sound advice, chat and never-ending enthusiasm for all things writerly. To my Cheltenham Critique Group, for encouragement, conversation and honest feedback. To The Suffolk Anthology bookshop, for providing a meeting space for our little group (and that all-important coffee and cake). To the Alliance of Independent Authors, for answering my sometimes ridiculous questions on publishing.

And lastly, to Julie, Bev, Tania, Kirsten and Kat who I 'met' through Alopecia UK. Thank you so much for bravely answering my questions on alopecia. This book wouldn't be the same without your input.

For help and advice on alopecia, please visit Alopecia UK at www.alopecia.org.uk.

About the Author

J. M. Forster is an award-winning writer of books for older children and young teens. She lives in Gloucestershire with her husband, two lovely sons and Frodo, the Australian labradoodle. *Bad Hair Days* is her second novel. Her first novel, *Shadow Jumper*, won Gold Award in the Wishing Shelf Book Awards 2014.

jm-forster.co.uk

jm-forster.com

Printed in Great Britain
by Amazon

34169870R00125